ANYTHING BUT Love

JACQUELINE HAYLEY

www.jacquelinehayley.com

First edition October 2016
This edition published June 2019

Editing by Amy Andrews
www.wordwitchery.com.au

Cover design by Alyssa Garcia
www.uplifting-designs.com

ISBN: 978-0-6485858-0-0

www.jacquelinehayley.com

To my husband, the love of my life.
Probably the only person I know who doesn't
want to read any of the sex scenes in this book.
Thank you for your support – it means everything.

And to Tam and Jill.
The best friends a girl could have.

CHAPTER 1

The increasingly loud banging on the front door had Sophie frozen. She'd been washing her favourite lace lingerie in the bathroom sink – because the washing machine had died last week – and now she stood, hand dripping on the tiles, her heart beating double time in her chest.

Right. Deep breath.

This couldn't be worse than the recent visit from her real estate agent, who had to personally deliver an eviction notice because she'd been refusing to acknowledge his emails. That had been particularly mortifying and, in the last couple of months, the mortifying moments had been stacking up.

For the tenth time that morning, she cursed her ex-fiancé. When she'd finally called off the engagement and left him, the charisma and bravado he'd been using to financially prop them up had crumbled, and the house of cards they had inhabited had rapidly fallen.

Six months later, the damn man had pulled a disappearing act, taking with him the last of the funds from their joint bank account. Most days, Sophie couldn't determine which emotion was stronger – anger or frustration. Unless you counted her willful blindness to the situation, none of this outcome was her doing, and she was struggling to make sense of her new reality.

"Damien where are you? You'd better make an appearance bloody soon," she muttered under her breath as she wiped her hands on her jeans and headed for the door, which was now rattling on its hinges under the onslaught of fist from the other side.

The sight that greeted her beyond the door's safety chain instantly caused her to take a step backwards, before rushing forward to slam it again. Too late, her guest thrust a large booted foot in the doorway and shouldered it open wide, snapping the so-called safety chain with ease.

"You must be Damien's missus," he stated, his eyes assessing and his mouth a mean line. "Thought I'd better pay you a visit, seeing as he's MIA and darlin', you better know he owes the big boss a lot of cash."

Sophie put a hand to her mouth to quell rising hysteria. Her visitor's eye glinted, his too-thin lips curling in a predatory grin.

She couldn't believe this was now her life. She was a university-educated 26-year old, with a coveted role on the graphic design team of a prestigious women's magazine. She was often in the social pages of Sydney's newspapers, especially after Damien had cemented their It-Couple status by proposing with a seriously large diamond.

Until Damien's gambling had gotten out of control, Sophie had enjoyed a standing appointment for a weekly wash and blow dry of her luxurious honey blonde locks, her nails were always impeccable and the staff at high-end boutique Belinda in Paddington knew her by name.

Life had turned from swanky to skanky with frightening speed and Sophie was way out of her depth.

"He's not here," she stuttered, taking another step back. "And we've broken up – we're not together anymore. Please, just give me your number and I'll pass it on to him."

"Darlin', he already has my number. And he's all out of

chances. He's racked up $420,000 and I'm here to collect."

He reached out a meaty finger and ran it down Sophie's cheek; "I'm pretty sure we can come to some sort of arrangement."

"Like fuck you can," came an angry growl as a large hand clamped down on the intruder's shoulder from behind. Sophie gasped and ran to dodge behind an armchair as shouts and expletives from both males burst forth.

Holy shit.

Sophie was so panicked it took her several moments to realise her rescuer was Robert, Damien's older brother.

What was he doing in Sydney?

He ran the family farm in the middle of god knows where. Sophie had never even met the guy and only recognised him from seeing a few old photos.

Regardless of her non-existent relationship with Robert, he was holding his own against the brutish thug, with both men trading blows equally. Sophie's heart lodged in her throat at the unleashed violence but with adrenaline surging she snatched up the table lamp beside her, coming around the armchair with it held high.

Clutching the heavy lamp base in sweaty hands she flicked her eyes back and forth between the men, waiting for an opportunity to strike, wondering if she had the guts to make it count.

Robert was easily six foot, his broad shoulders were bunched with hard muscle and he obviously knew enough about street fighting. Before Sophie could act, he had knocked the other man to the ground and shoved his cowboy-booted foot against the throat of the fallen man.

"I don't know what the hell you're doing here, but don't

think for a moment you're coming anywhere near her again."

——

Robert's fists remained clenched as he glared down uncompromisingly. He ground his foot down a little harder. "Do. You. Understand?"

The haze of fury that had descended when he'd arrived to find the thug at Sophie's door began to recede. He rolled his shoulders back to ease some tension, but didn't break eye contact. The idea of Sophie in danger was a physical pain, and he redirected it to power the thick muscles of his legs.

The thug grunted and started to thrash his legs, signaling he wasn't getting enough air. With reluctance, Robert removed his foot but stood threateningly, positioning himself between Sophie – who was watching wide-eyed and shaking – and the downed man.

"Get out. And don't ever come back."

The thug was bleeding from the nose and mouth, and getting to all fours he spat a string of bloody saliva onto the carpet. Stumbling to his feet he leered at Sophie, "I'll be seeing you later darlin', and I can't wait to get to know you better."

Fighting to restrain his anger, Robert grabbed the back of the man's shirt and shoved him through the door, firmly closing it behind him. Slowly, he turned to face his brother's fiancé. Now was *not* the time to wonder why he'd been so worked up over a woman he'd never met before. Hell, worked up didn't really describe the blind murderous rage he'd felt, but again, that was something he didn't need to concentrate on right now.

"What the hell was that?" He sounded angrier than he'd intended, and he winced internally as Sophie's knees buckled. Striding to her side, he eased her into the armchair. Her head didn't quite reach the top of his chest and her slight figure curved unconsciously into his body.

Damn if she didn't feel amazing in his arms.

Sophie stared up at him wordlessly, and he momentarily got lost in green eyes and long, thick eyelashes. Right before he mentally shook himself. Jesus, was he really attracted to his brother's fiancé? He needed to get a grip.

He was here to speak to his brother. The little shit wasn't answering his phone, but if he thought he could risk Robert's future on the farm and not expect a visit from his big brother, then he had another thing coming.

And as pretty as Sophie might be, no doubt she was elbow deep in the mess Damien was making.

The two brother's each owned half of the 7,000-acre property their parents had left them when they'd been killed in a car accident while the boys were still at boarding school, but only Robert had shouldered the responsibility of it. Damien had chosen to remain in Sydney and hadn't set foot on their land since the day after their parent's funeral, while Robert had given up his own dreams of a university education to keep the farm operating.

He hadn't been able to stomach the thought of land that had been in their family for three generations being sold. And besides, even with an agronomy degree under his belt, he'd been intending on returning home regardless.

Turns out he didn't need an agronomy degree to make a success of the enterprise. At the ripe old age of 28 he had a business many seasoned farmers were envious of. Which made the sting of Damien's underhand dealings cut deeper.

"Are you okay? What the hell was that guy doing here?"

"Looking for Damien." Her voice was small and she didn't make eye contact.

"Sophie, where is Damien?" he asked, crouching his large frame in front of the armchair. In the face of her continued silence, he placed a finger under her chin and gently forced her gaze to met his own. "I need to know. And from what I just witnessed, you need to know too."

"I don't know. I really don't," she all-but whispered. "Ever since we broke up he's been sketchy with communication, and then he sent a text saying he had to take off for a while and I haven't heard anything from him for over three weeks."

"I don't understand how you can't not know where he is," Robert ran a hand through his hair in frustration. "Hang on, you broke up? Last I heard you were getting married."

At this rate, the creases in his forehead were going to become permanent. He was as confused as hell and had to wonder how much truth was coming out of her pretty little mouth. Was this an act to cover up any involvement she had in Damien siphoning money from the farm's bank account?

"I told you, we're not together. It's not my job to keep tabs on him anymore. He's been spiraling out of control and I wanted out – he's not the same man he was. He emptied our bank account and now I'm being evicted and I don't know how I'm meant to move all my furniture, or even where I'm going to move it to… and the bread is mouldy," she finished tremulously, a tear sliding down her smooth cheek.

Ah hell. This was definitely not what Robert had anticipated.

CHAPTER 2

"I can't believe I opened the door to him," Sophie said quietly. Seriously, what had she been thinking? Obviously it hadn't been a neighbor popping by for a cup of sugar. She shook herself mentally and eased back in the armchair, more to get some distance from Robert than for comfort.

The man was *big*. He filled all her personal space, and then some. And she was still reeling from the shock of almost being molested by her ex-fiancé's loan shark. Or loan shark's moneyman. Or enforcer.

Or whatever the hell he'd been.

"You can't stay here," Robert stated.

"Well that's obvious," she snapped, then she sighed; "Sorry, I didn't mean to be rude. Thank you. So much. I don't know what I would have done if you hadn't have shown up when you did." She paused. "Why *did* you show up?"

Robert rocked back on his heels and then, gracefully for his size, rose to a standing position and took a few steps back. He seemed to be measuring her words and then he, too, sighed.

"Damien's taken money out of the farm, and now he's talking to the bank about selling up his share."

Sophie groaned and dropped her head into her hands. "He just keeps fucking up," she mumbled.

Sophie had been fresh out of uni when she'd met Damien at a bar one Friday evening; he'd swept her off her feet with his extravagant affection, lavish gifts and his fast lifestyle; it was all Bellini cocktails at Randwick Races, yacht parties on the harbor, exclusive invites to the city's hot spots, and high-flying friends who talked a big talk.

Estranged from her own family and craving any kind of connection, she'd been dazzled by his charm and quick wit. Their crazy love affair swung into high gear and hadn't slowed down. Well, not until his recreational drug habit and gambling turned into a major problem.

And when Sophie had finally taken a good hard look at their relationship and her life, she knew she had to get out. Damien wasn't the man she'd fallen in love with, and when she'd tried to discuss it with him, he'd told her to go to hell.

It was just all so sordid and *dirty*. She was the girl who bought $400 heels in her lunch break and spent the equivalent of a small African nation's GDP at her local drycleaners.

Even her closest friend, Sara, didn't know the extent of what Sophie had been reduced to since Damien had absconded with their savings. It had become a matter of whether she spent her few remaining dollars on a train ticket to work, or bought food. Lucky it was considered an advantage to be thin in the magazine industry.

"Shit, Sara. I was meant to call her back." Sophie remembered, grabbing her phone and dialing. "I'm sorry, I just need to make this call." Robert's jaw ticked but he stayed silent.

Sophie desperately needed her monthly pay cheque from her job, but Paul, her fiercely territorial, flamboyantly gay Art Director – who took credit for everyone else's work – was making her question her desire to stay with the magazine.

So it was imperative that she was debriefed about last

night's after work drinks from Sara – who was the Beauty Editor. Sara had planned on straight up asking Paul about the juicy promotion he kept dangling in front of Sophie. And money was now the name of the game.

The phone only rang once before Sara's breathless voice answered; "I'm on my way, with coffee. Paul's a complete bitch and I think we need to seriously start looking at different job options for you. I'm two seconds away."

Great. Now she needed a new home *and* a new job.

Sara had a key to her house and the door swung open yet again as the bubbly blonde burst through, only to stop abruptly at the sight of Robert.

"Well hello there. If I knew I was going to be meeting a Tall Dark Handsome Stranger I'd have worn nicer underwear," Sara's eyebrows raised as she looked appreciatively over an unmoving, and unimpressed, Robert.

She swung her gaze to Sophie and her eyebrows raised even higher. "Honey, what's wrong? Is there a problem?" Her eyes shifted back to Robert.

"No, no. It's fine. Well, not really, but Robert is okay," she assured her friend.

"I'd say a little more than okay," mused Sara, practically licking her lips and flashing an overly bright smile.

Hmmm. Why did Sophie's gut do a funny twisty thing when another female showed interest in her *ex-fiancé's brother*. Right, reality check. Damien and Robert couldn't be more physically different from each other. Sophie was definitely NOT attracted to him. He'd just been her knight in shining armor, that was all. And back to that.

"I haven't been completely level with you, Sar. You know that Damien and I broke off the engagement, but now he's

taken off with all our money and I don't know where he is."
Saying those words, and facing up to reality, was hard, and
Sophie choked up.

Luckily Sara wasn't her best friend for nothing. She had
Sophie wrapped up in a hug before she could burst into tears.

"Okay you, spill," she commanded.

"Before we get to that, I think it's time we called the
police," Robert said firmly, pulling out his mobile phone.

"What? Is that really necessary? I wasn't hurt…" Sophie
pulled away from Sara. Her heart had calmed back to its
normal rhythm and as each minute passed she felt more and
more removed from the craziness that had just occurred.

"I'll call Damien and tell him to work it out. He's not my
problem any more."

Robert's voice was hard; "And how's that been going,
trying to get in contact with him? Because I know he's sure
as hell not answering my calls. And that thug is making it
your problem. He just broke into your home, threatened you
and assaulted me."

"I think you may have kinda assaulted him a little more
than he did you…"

"It was self-defense Sophie. And what would have
happened if I hadn't been here?"

She couldn't suppress a shudder.

Sara stamped her foot to get their attention, her hands on
her hips and her eyes wide. "What the hell *did* happen here?"

———

It was something else to witness the bond of friendship

between these two women, and Robert watched with reluctant fascination as Sara extracted the whole sorry tale, all the while inserting comfort, encouragement and expletives at the correct times.

It turns out there was a lot he hadn't known about his little brother, starting with the drug addiction which apparently he refused to get help with, denying there was a problem at all.

Robert was blasted with a bitter-tasting flash of guilt that he hadn't kept better tabs on his sibling. His temples throbbed as the guilt joined the anger and frustration he was already battling.

Having moved to sit on another armchair, he checked his watch and restrained himself from interrupting. Time was something he valued and treated accordingly, and so far nothing this morning had gone to plan.

He'd known it was possible he wouldn't see Damien and, although driving eight hours to the city and not getting an explanation was damn frustrating, he was now more concerned about the welfare of his almost-sister-in-law.

Sara glanced with irritation at his tapping foot, but was distracted by the arrival of two men in blue. "I do like a man in uniform," she mock-whispered to no one in particular.

Robert was grateful the police officers were taking the call out seriously, although it was concerning how interested they were in Damien's financial affairs.

One of them stepped out to make a call back to the station and on returning explained that Damien's name had triggered a red flag – it appeared some of his recent financial transactions may not have been aboveboard, and hadn't gone undetected by law enforcement.

"We'll be in touch, and we're going to do everything we

can from our end, but I'd strongly advise you not to stay here. Have you got somewhere safe to go? Even better if you could get out of the city; these men mean business, and the further you are away from them, the better," said the younger of the two policemen as they were leaving.

The door swung closed, leaving the three of them sitting in silence, which Sophie eventually broke. "Shit. What do I do now?"

"You'll come to my apartment of course. I know it's only one bedroom, but we've shared a bed before. It'll be fun to have a roomie," Sara replied immediately.

"You're coming home with me." It was more statement, than question, and out of his mouth before he'd had time to evaluate the reasoning behind the idea.

Both Sophie and Sara stopped mid conversation and stared at him – he suspected Sara had almost forgotten his presence. But he realised he wanted, no *needed*, Sophie to be safe with him. It was a logical plan that would solve many of her current issues.

And, he admitted to himself, possibly draw Damien back to the farm so they could sort out their own problems.

"We'll pack up and fit what we can in my ute, and you'll just have to leave the rest," he said, glancing around at what was obviously an expensively decorated interior.

"You've got to be kidding," Sophie exclaimed. "I know you're Damien's brother but I barely know you. And I can't just leave everything behind, that's insane."

"You're the one who said you didn't know how you were going to move everything, or where it was going to go. You're getting evicted, remember?" it wasn't a gentle reminder, and that throb in his temple stepped up a notch.

"What's insane is some thug trying to hurt you," broke in Sara quietly. "I think he's right. I think you need to get out of the city for a while. At least until you hear from Damien. And I can pack up the house and organise storage, don't worry about that."

Sophie looked between the two of them and he was slightly mollified to know he wasn't the only one with mounting frustration. "Well what about my job? I can't just up and leave!"

"Honey, you hate your job. Paul drives you crazy and you know you wouldn't have lasted there much longer. Think of this as a chance to catch your breath and see what other jobs are out there."

So the blonde bombshell was on his side. Good to know. And time to press his advantage. "Where are your suitcases? It's a long drive back to the farm, we're going to need to leave sooner rather than later."

It had been later rather than sooner before Sophie and Sara had packed up most of what was deemed too important to leave, and not before Robert had put his foot down about her bringing actual furniture.

"I might live in the sticks, but my house *is* furnished." He didn't miss Sophie's wistful look around the house and felt a tiny pang of remorse, but the tray on his ute was already nearing the legal weight limit.

The trip so far had been quiet; Sophie had dozed off with her legs propped up on the dashboard. Robert was struggling to keep his eyes off those legs; with her narrow shoulders and small waist she appeared smaller than she was, even with those endlessly long legs.

She had curves in all the right places and when she sighed in her sleep Robert's lap started to feel a little uncomfortable.

"My brother's girl," he chanted under his breath.

Due to traffic, they were still a good four hours from the farm when night fell and, with it, a ferocious Summer storm. It was the frantic swiping of the windscreen wipers that woke Sophie.

"Sorry, I've been lousy company. I completely crashed."

"No problems, but I think we're going to have to pull over for the night. The radio just said there's flash flooding in the next town, and I'm pretty beat myself."

"Okay, sure. Where are we, anyway? I've never come west of the mountains before."

He raised an eyebrow at her, and then turned his gaze back to the road. "City girl through and through huh? Must be what Damien likes about you – he hated the rural life." Robert shifted his eyes back to Sophie quickly, "he may also have appreciated your snoring."

"My what? I don't snore," she protested indignantly, before sticking the tip of her tongue out at him. And damn if the sight of her pink tongue didn't have his lap feeling uncomfortable again.

"You may have other attributes he appreciates that I haven't witnessed yet," he conceded, and then he clenched the steering wheel a little tighter as he realised the innuendo he'd just made.

Definitely time to get off the road and out of a confined space with this woman.

CHAPTER 3

It was like a scene out of a cheesy chick flick – *of course*
the motel wouldn't have two rooms available. Instead, they
were bunking down in a room with two single beds. Which,
Sophie had to concede, was better than a room with just
one big bed – she definitely didn't need to think about how
uncomfortable that scenario would have been.

Robert was braving the elements to bring their luggage
in, and Sophie was grateful for the opportunity to get a little
space from him. It wasn't that his company was unpleasant,
quite the opposite. It was just she kept having the most
inconvenient hot flushes when their hands brushed while
adjusting the radio station, or he looked at her from under his
inky eyelashes for just a beat too long.

It was like she could literally feel her heart thumping too
hard and fast when she was in close proximity to him – he
was more male than she'd encountered in a long time. Hell,
in ever.

While Damien was just an inch or two taller than her and
his lean frame looked fabulous in a bespoke suit, he hadn't
ever dwarfed her the way Robert's sheer bulk did. Robert
made her feel feminine and protected and god damn *achy*.

Which was completely insane and something Sophie
needed to shake off real quick; this is what happened when
your sex life had petered out to non-existent because your
ex-fiancé was either too out of it on drugs, or just not around.

And it wasn't like she'd dated in the last six months.

Sophie slumped onto the nearest bed and looked around. Non-descript was too big a word to explain the extreme plainness of the motel room, and it sure as hell wasn't giving her a reprieve from her thoughts. Because if she were being honest with herself, she'd acknowledge that she'd never before experienced this frission of desire, not even in the heady early days of her relationship with Damien. And she sure as hell didn't know what to do about it.

Robert set down her suitcase and his duffle bag, shaking water drops from his shaggy, dark hair. "It's really coming down out there," he commented.

"Mmm hmmm," Sophie was distracted by his t-shirt clinging to his broad chest and was actually thinking the rain was all kinds of miraculous right about now.

"This is the blue suitcase you meant, right?"

She glanced at the luggage he was referring to and shook her head. "Um, no. That's actually not it…" She hoped if she looked apologetic enough he'd take pity on her and go and haul back the tarp covering the tray of his ute again to find the one she needed.

"Well what's in here then? Clothes are clothes, right?"

"That suitcase is just my, umm, my lingerie."

"You have a whole suitcase of underwear?" he was incredulous and slightly amused. Amusement won out. "You seriously have enough pairs of undies to fill this whole suitcase?" He reached out to unzip it and Sophie sprang in front of it, as though ready to defend it with her life.

Every girl had a thing. Some went mad for lip gloss, some had a Carrie Bradshaw-worthy shoe fetish. For her, it was lingerie. The frilly, lacy, not-always-comfortable but *always* delicious kind. "Yes, this whole thing. Don't judge me, it's my one weakness and I didn't want to risk it getting eaten by mice or moths in storage."

"You only have one weakness?" There goes that raised eyebrow again, although this time his mouth quirked up in a smile. His full, sensuous lips were perfectly complemented by a defined chin and chiseled jaw, and an elusive dimple appeared beneath his day-old stubble.

"Well I want to see this suitcase full of underwear. Come on, 'fess up."

This jokey, cheeky side of Robert was unexpected, and Sophie realised she had no clue about his personality. All she really knew was that he could handle himself in a dangerous situation and that he made her pulse race. To be honest, she'd never really thought about him at all; Damien didn't like to talk about his country childhood or his family, and due to the stilted relationship between the brothers she'd never had the opportunity to met Robert.

"Not a chance. Even Damien doesn't know the full extent of my lingerie indulgence – I think he'd be horrified by the amount of money I've spent, and for him to be concerned about spending money on expensive things… well, it says something."

She could tell immediately that the mention of his brother hit home for Robert. The grin left his face and his eyes lost their twinkle. She realised she liked putting that mischievous glint there.

"You're right. Probably shouldn't be asking to see my brother's fiancé's lingerie collection," his voice was flat. "Maybe you should try calling him again."

"*Ex*-fiancé. And I've already left him four messages today, plus I'm sure the police have left a few of their own. I'll try again in the morning. I think I'm going to take a shower."

"Okay. I'll try and find your *other* blue suitcase," he couldn't get out of the room quick enough and Sophie closed her eyes in frustration. WHY was he getting to her?

The suitcase full of lingerie was like an elephant in the room. Robert couldn't look at it, but it seemed to be always in his peripheral vision. What he wouldn't give to have just a glimpse of its contents. Preferably on Sophie. Jesus Christ he needed to get a handle on his libido because ex or not, this woman was off-limits.

Maybe he shouldn't have turned down Cindy's offer of a quick shag against the back wall of the pub last weekend. But if she didn't want to commit to a proper relationship with him then he was through with the 'you scratch my itch and I'll scratch yours' arrangement they had going on.

He was ready to settle down and, while it wasn't an all-consuming bright-burning passion with Cindy, they got along well and he liked her. Really liked her. She was his people. Born and bred in the country, she understood the lifestyle. Not to mention she had an exceptional rack.

Their mutually convenient 'friendship' had been enough for Robert to start with, but he was over it just being a quick fuck. He wanted more. It was just a shame his libido didn't have the same morals.

Sophie was on the phone ordering room service, her legs curled under her and a few drops of water still clinging to her neck from the shower. Robert doubted she knew her nipples were tempting shadows beneath her snug-fitting white singlet, but his throat went dry at the sight of them.

"I'm kind of skeptical about ordering Chinese takeaway from the front desk, because they were clearly *not* Asian, but the only other option was sandwiches. Okay with you?"

He knew what he'd really like to be eating right now, and it sure as hell wasn't food. If his lap had been uncomfortable in the vehicle, it was nothing compared to the throb in his cock now. All that talk of lingerie, and she wasn't wearing a bra? Even the sight of lace would be more calming than the rosy nipples on show.

The sweet torment of seeing her like this, when she had no idea how turned on he was, was driving him insane – making him seriously question his judgment in bringing her into his home. "My brother's girl," he muttered wrenching his eyes away and flicking on the television.

"What did you say?"

"Nothing. Chinese is good. Great. I'm starving."

It made him oddly happy they'd agreed on not watching a reality TV show, and instead sat in companionable silence watching a British cop show until their food arrived. It made him happier still to see how eager Sophie was in devouring it; he liked a girl who could eat with abandon. It made him wonder what else she'd do with abandon…

So yeah, one more night with Cindy definitely wasn't off the cards, although he couldn't muster a lot of enthusiasm at the thought. Cindy's abundant cleavage had lost its allure, and in its place he was imaging what Sophie would look like without that damn singlet.

Cock, throbbing. "I'm going to have a shower."

CHAPTER 4

Sophie hadn't thought she'd sleep a wink, knowing that Robert lay mere centimeters away from her. She'd lain in bed with the sheet tucked under her chin, trying to even her breath and ignore her body's state of high alert over the man in the next bed.

In spite of that, she fell quickly into a deep sleep – the drama of the day ebbing away to, strangely, a sense of security.

Robert had been up and dressed by the time she'd woken and surprisingly there was no awkwardness between them. She'd quickly brushed her teeth and swept her hair into a messy bun on top of her head and was ready to hit the road in no time.

She smiled secretly at Robert expressing surprise at how low-fuss she was. Little did he know the preparation she went through before walking into the office of a glossy magazine every morning… driving to the tiny town of Minnippi – population 1,300 – didn't require a double coat of mascara.

In fact, curled into the seat of Robert's ute wearing her favourite Sass & Bide jeans, a comfortable grey marle t-shirt and a pair of aviator sunglasses she'd picked up at the last service station, Sophie was feeling a strange sense of liberation.

"It's kind of nice, to get away from it all. I guess I can understand why Damien just took off like he did, not that it doesn't still make me furious – it's just like him to bail instead of trying to sort things out. I really do appreciate you doing this for me."

"Well, you're practically family. And there was no way you were staying there, when that creep is sure to turn up again."

Sophie noticed him flex his fingers on the steering wheel and knew he'd been more rattled by what could have happened than he let on.

So much had happened so quickly since then, she hadn't really had a chance to process it herself. Thinking about it now, she was flooded once again by her anger at Damien for putting her in the situation. Coupled with the ever-present anxiety about money, before she knew it tears were slipping quietly down her cheeks. So much for that weightless liberation.

Embarrassed, she fisted the tears from her eyes and set the aviators back in place, hoping that Robert hadn't noticed.

Without looking at her, he flicked the blinkers on and pulled over onto the side of the road. They were surrounded on all sides by endless golden paddocks of recently harvested wheat stalks, and the road meandered ahead without pretension.

Sophie surreptitiously sniffed, and then looked at him with faux brightness. "Why are we pulling over?"

"Want to talk about it?"

She sighed. Of course he'd noticed. Damien would have too, the only difference being that Damien would have pretended not to, because it was easier to ignore silly things like emotions.

"There's not much to say Robert. I broke off my engagement, some thug thinks I can pay a $420,000 gambling debt that doesn't belong to me, and I've walked out on my job. Life's fucking great."

"You're safe with me." Robert's gaze was intent on hers as he reached for her hands. "I'm serious Sophie, I won't let anyone hurt you."

"Not even your brother?"

She wouldn't miss her high society lifestyle, not really, but she'd trusted that Damien would be her happy ever after – she wanted that commitment and security. She needed it.

All her life she'd struggled to find her place in the world. Her older brother was the golden boy and she never quite measured up – something her parents didn't hide from her, and the main reason she didn't feel she could turn to them now.

They'd moved suburbs several times during her childhood, resulting in different schools and, despite her natural affability she'd struggled to forge close friendships. She was the one everyone was friends with, but she hadn't had a best friend, until Sara.

Her social life at university had been tempered by her need to prove to her parents she could be a success, and she spent more nights at the library than in a nightclub. Not that her parents cared, or even noticed.

And then Damien had seen something in her, and swept her into his orbit. She'd always known she wasn't her true self when she was with him – she was who he wanted her to be. And she was happy enough to sacrifice that part of herself if it meant she belonged.

Which was laughable now, when she belonged nowhere and was sitting on the side of a country road with a man she didn't know. It was time to reevaluate what she wanted with her life, and become who *she* wanted to be.

"Look, it doesn't matter. Let's just keep going, the sooner we get there the better."

"It's upsetting you so it does matter Sophie. What can I do?" His deep, concerned voice brought on a new wave of tears.

"You're doing it. Take me to your home."

———

Robert spent the next two hours of the drive mentally beating his little brother up. Completely separate from the fact he was trying to screw Robert over with the farm, it was unfathomable how he could have let Sophie go.

Robert thought it a scumbag action to leave any woman in a mess like the one Damien had made, but to leave *Sophie…*

Fucking madness. She had the face of a goddess and a body that was slowly driving him to distraction. And she was sweet as hell.

Lord knew if he'd ever had a woman like that in his arms, he sure as hell wouldn't be letting her go.

As if on cue, his phone beeped with an incoming text message.

Cindy: Hey hot stuff. Missed you this weekend. Will I see you at Wilko's barbeque on Friday night?

Robert took a sidelong glance at Sophie and didn't reply.

"We're about to drive into Minnippi, and my farm is 50-kilometers the other side. Do you want anything in town before we head out?"

Sophie just shook her head, interested eyes scanning the dusty landscape. The vehicle's air-conditioner had them at a comfortable 22 degrees, but Robert knew the dry heat outside was going to feel like it was sucking oxygen away from the un-acclimatized Sophie.

Arriving at noon in the middle of a particularly brutal Summer wasn't exactly welcoming, but if Sophie was going to stick it out here for any length of time then she was going to have to toughen up.

Robert was fortunate that Acacia Ridge, his property, was situated on the local river and several of his paddocks were irrigated; these irrigated lucerne crops were what sustained his fledgling Black Angus cattle stud. The sea of green was also a welcome sight as they drove through his front gate, which was flanked by two enormous cedar trees.

"Wow. It's… big."

Robert grinned at Sophie's understatement. He was proud that he'd not only managed to hold onto the family farm, but also ensured the business thrived. He'd kept up the traditional cropping practices, while turning his focus to the Black Angus market, which was receiving favourable attention from the restaurant industry.

As they pulled around behind the sprawling farmhouse with its well-maintained edging of agapanthus, a cloud of dust followed them up the driveway. "Company already," he said, shading his eyes against the harsh sun to follow the path of the oncoming vehicle.

"Stay inside the cab until it's pulled up, otherwise you'll get covered in dust."

The Hilux drew to a halt beside them and his neighbor

John Wilkinson – Wilko – jumped out. Always high-energy, he was more enthusiastic than usual upon seeing Robert had company.

"Well hi there darlin', welcome to the ranch." Eyes locked on Sophie he moved past Robert and grabbed her hand to help her down.

It pissed Robert off.

"I think she can get down by herself Wilko, she's a big girl."

"She's a tiny angel, is what she is. Where did you find her?" he demanded of Robert, finally taking his eyes off Sophie.

Robert rounded the vehicle in long strides so he was standing in front of Wilko. "She's my brother's fiancé, so hands off."

Ignoring Robert's gruff tone, Sophie smiled around him at Wilko. "Sorry about the caveman. I'm Sophie, Damien's ex-fiancé, it's nice to meet you."

"Where's the prodigal son then?" asked Wilko.

Robert and Wilko exchanged a glance. Wilko was well aware of the strained relationship between the brothers, and Robert knew he'd never heard mention of Sophie before.

"Never mind angel, I was just up on the stock route when I saw you drive past, and thought I'd call down to make sure Rob was coming to my barbeque on Friday. And now that I've met you, I've decided the night is now in your honour."

"Laying it on a bit thick, aren't you mate? I don't reckon Michelle would take too kindly to that."

"Settle down, I'm just messin' with you. Michelle would have my balls with rusty shears and I know it. But you should both come, bring some beer and I'll see you at seven." With that, he loped back to his vehicle and pulled away, waving a careless arm out the window.

"Well he's a whirlwind."

"He's courting trouble is what he is."

Sophie looked up at him coyly, "Don't tell me you're getting territorial?"

Robert ground his teeth together. If she had *any* idea just how territorial he was feeling she'd run a mile. He'd be putting the word out in no uncertain terms that she was off-limits. To everyone.

CHAPTER 5

The interior of the weatherboard house was deliciously cool and Sophie sighed with relief as she toed off her designer sneakers and looked around the room Robert had shown her to.

It was bright and airy, with French doors that opened onto a wrap-around verandah. The wrought iron bed looked antique and had a simple white linen doona and was stacked with plump pillows that were practically begging her to lay her head on them.

Instead, she eyed the rather large pile of her luggage that was heaped near the door and began to methodically unpack the contents carefully hanging them away. She had expensive taste when it came to fashion, but she was also fastidious about caring for it.

She hadn't grown up with an excess of money and so hadn't taken the easy money of Damien's lifestyle for granted. Not that that had served her well in the long run.

Coming across a casual sundress she shrugged out of her jeans and was pulling her t-shirt over her head when she felt a prickle run down her back. Gasping, she twirled to face the door and came face to face with Robert, leaning against the doorframe with his arms crossed over his broad chest.

"If you'd prefer some privacy, I'd advise on closing the door in future," he smirked.

A hot blush spread across her face. She knew exactly how

her creamy lace Brazilian panties looked cupping her ass –
they were a favourite for a reason.

"Seriously?! You couldn't knock?"

Am I pissed off, or – weirdly – turned on?

"Like I said, the door was open. I just came to see if you
needed anything."

"I'm fine. And I'll remember to close the door in future,"
she muttered drily.

He stepped back neatly as she shut the door in his face
and, panting, leaned back against it, clutching her t-shirt to
her chest.

He'd smirked at her. She hadn't imagined the heat in his
eyes or the way they'd lazily travelled up her body. And it
was damn sexy. What the hell had happened to the slightly
standoff-ish man who'd only brought her here out of a sense
of duty to his little brother?

From the moment he'd entered her apartment in Sydney
he'd been confident and assured, but this man had been more
than that. *Way* more. He'd practically oozed sex.

What the hell?

It was her grumbling stomach that eventually forced Sophie
to leave her room and seek out the kitchen.

While she was still flustered over their earlier encounter,
what unnerved her was her own reaction. She *liked* knowing
he'd appreciated the view, and the warmth that had pooled
between her legs had been slightly shocking.

She didn't consider herself an overly sexual person; sure,
she enjoyed sex as much as the next girl, but that kind of
reaction from just a *look* had never happened before.

Regardless, a girl had to eat, and maybe Robert wouldn't even be in the house. He had mentioned he needed to see his farmhand to check how the irrigation was going and about moving some stock. Sophie got the feeling he was hands-on with the management of the property, and didn't often have time away.

Her stomach fluttered traitorously when she entered the kitchen to find him sorting through a stack of mail. He looked up and gave her a slow, lazy smile.

"I'm just making a coffee, want one?"

"Oh god I'd kill for one," she replied, eyeing the fancy-looking cappuccino-maker on the counter and grateful for his attempt at normalcy – the sooner they forgot about that moment in her bedroom doorway the better.

"So, about earlier…" his back was to her as he expertly worked the coffee machine. Damn. Blood rushed to stain her face again and she squirmed inwardly. It was beyond awkward that he'd seen her half naked.

"I crossed a boundary, and I'm sorry. I should have walked away when I realised you were undressing."

"Yeah, that would have been the polite thing to do." She raised an eyebrow – best to keep it light. And *definitely* best to ignore that sudden trace of disappointment. The flare of regret confused her, it's not like she wanted him to be attracted to her. *Right?*

"And if you could keep your door closed when you're getting naked, that would make this whole co-habitation thing easier."

"Door closed from now on. Got it."

He passed her a mug frothing with milk and as their fingertips brushed she swore she felt a jolt of pleasure, unconsciously pressing her thighs together in response.

She took a sip and sighed in exaggerated ecstasy. "This coffee is really good. I was thinking I was going to miss the barista at my usual café, but you could give him a run for his money."

"I aim to please."

And didn't that get a girl thinking a whole lot of inappropriate thoughts. Although wondering what kind of lover this man would be was *not* conducive to living together harmoniously. Seriously, he was he ex's brother, and it wasn't like she was going to be here at the farm for long.

Flustered, she took another sip of her coffee and then almost choked as her eyes snagged on the milk container sitting on the bench. Jumping up she ran for the sink and spat out her mouthful.

"What the hell?" Robert watched her with mild alarm, his own coffee raised halfway to his mouth.

"Don't drink it! The milk is bad!"

"What are you talking about? The milk is fine. See?" He took a long swallow and smacked his lips together, mimicking her earlier exaggerated appreciation.

"It's out of date." Abandoning her mug on the sink, she grabbed up the milk and held it out to him. "The use by date was a month ago," she screwed up her mouth and could swear her taste buds were literally shriveling on her tongue. She was surprised her stomach hadn't already revolted.

"Did it taste fine?"

"Yes, but –"

"That's because it is fine. Living so far out of town, I don't get to the supermarket to get groceries every week. So I freeze bread and milk and defrost them as I need them."

He was watching her with quirked eyebrows, and Sophie slowly lowered the milk container until it was hanging by her side, willing herself not to blush in embarrassment again.

That hadn't been an overreaction – she just hadn't been fully informed. If the milk *was* bad, then he'd be gagging over the kitchen sink too, instead of laughing at her.

"You freeze your milk?"

"It's probably more habit than anything else – my mum used to do it. Back when we were kids, we probably only got to town once a month. Don't worry," he added, seeing the look of surprise on Sophie's face, "I get to town a little more often than that now. But it's always good to be prepared. The deep freeze is always fully stocked."

Sophie had known that living on a farm was going to take some getting used to. But small practicalities like this were completely foreign to her. No wonder Robert had asked on their way here whether she needed anything, it wasn't like there was a 7-Eleven she could duck out to.

It was a whole other lifestyle out here in the country.

"Anything else I should be aware of?"

He grinned at her as he finished his coffee. "How do you feel about frogs?"

"Frogs?"

"The little buggers come up through the septic – it's wise to check the toilet before you use it, so you don't get a surprise."

Her voice was weak. 'That's…"

"Life."

Lowering herself onto a kitchen stool, she vowed she would *not* scream if she saw a frog in the toilet. She'd played the damsel in distress in front of Robert quite enough, thank you very much. She could handle a frog. Surely.

"So what do I do, if there is a, frog, in the toilet?"

"Just give it a flush. But be conscious of water usage, okay? We're on rainwater here, and if it doesn't rain soon, we'll be getting low."

Oh yeah, she was *way* out of her depth here. This wasn't another lifestyle, this was a whole other world.

———

Robert had been mentally berating himself ever since Sophie had closed the bedroom door in his face. Confusion didn't come close to describing the roiling emotions that had settled in his gut.

He wanted her. Bad. But the guilt of wanting his brother's girl swamped him, and he still didn't trust that she wasn't involved with Damien's underhand scheming to sell the farm.

Besides that, she was so completely not what he was looking for in a woman. He wanted a partner not just in the bedroom, but outdoors as well. Farming was his life, and his future wife needed to be comfortable with everything that came with that. Not that he was thinking Sophie could ever be his wife. Hell, she was only going to be here a couple of days, a week at the most.

That was why Cindy would be perfect; she'd grown up on a farm and wasn't afraid to get her hands dirty. And so what that he didn't have that hot flare of sexual awareness with her? Sex with Cindy was good. And what they lacked in passion, they made up for in compatibility.

But then Sophie had walked into the kitchen in that floaty

sundress, smelling of vanilla, and compatibility was the last thing on his mind.

Nope, all he could picture was the intimate curve of her back and the sweet swell of her ass in that lace underwear, right before she'd spun around and caught him looking. As soon as he'd realised she wasn't dressed he should have backed away, he wasn't a creep. But his body had had other ideas and he'd reacted accordingly.

So maybe he was a creep.

He wasn't proud of the way he'd smirked, or the way his eyes had greedily devoured her. Decency had been damned and his only thought was of getting closer. It was just as well she'd closed the door in his face, because he'd been fine with coveting something that wasn't his.

And she wasn't his. Not by a long shot.

Which didn't stop a grin stretching across his face as she struggled to contain her horror of potential amphibian invaders.

Teasing her about the reality of life on the farm shouldn't be a turn on, it should be reinforcing exactly how unsuited she was to his life. But the way her lips were set in a pout of distaste just made him want to see how soft they were. To nip at that bottom lip until she opened for him. A groan caught in his throat and he hastily set down his coffee mug.

This was madness, and he needed to get away from her before he couldn't help himself from tasting that mouth of hers.

"I need to go and check some stock. I'll be back in a couple of hours," his voice was huskier than he liked, but he guessed that's what happened when you repressed your body's urges.

Stalking out onto the back verandah he barely paused to

tug on his work boots, heading straight for the farm bike. He needed to ride hard and fast with the wind in his face to get her half-naked body out of his head; to get his priorities back in order.

Rosie, his faithful Kelpie, came loping up behind him and with a whistled command from her master she bounded up in front of him – sitting on the bike's fuel tank. With a spray of gravel he tore down the driveway, no direction in mind except to outrace his own desires.

His chest tightened thinking of Damien, the little brother he'd grown up with. They'd climbed trees together, chased kangaroos on their dirt bikes, swam at the weir and wrestled as hard as they'd laughed. They were brothers. Boarding school had put some distance between them, with two years separating their classes, but it wasn't until the death of their parents and Damien's decision to stay in the city that they'd truly started to drift apart.

Robert struggled to understand that someone who'd been raised with the same values and morals as he had could have chosen to live the lifestyle that Damien thrived in.

His head pounded, still trying to make sense of the fact his brother, his blood, was trying to sell half the farm without even discussing it with him. And the gambling debt? What the hell had he been thinking?

More than that, Robert felt his blood boil thinking of the danger Damien had so carelessly placed Sophie in. How he could have left her in such a callous manner was beyond Robert's comprehension.

He'd known the woman for less than 48 hours and she'd already turned his world upside down. He was starting to seriously doubt he could continue to deny the attraction between them.

Which was insane. It didn't matter that her and Damien weren't together anymore. An ex was still off-limits between brothers.

And that was the kicker, wasn't it? Could he trust her word that she'd called off the engagement? Or was it a convenient way of escaping any blame now that Robert was wanting answers for Damien trying to sell the farm.

Was Sophie in on the scheme?

He pulled up short at that thought, and then coasted the bike to a stop next to a fallen tree log on the dam bank. Climbing off he stretched out on the log with Rosie contentedly beside him, absently rubbing her ears.

Regardless of her motives, he hadn't been this turned on since he'd had Mandy O'Sullivan pressed up against the gym wall when he was 15. And he hadn't even *touched* Sophie.

"It's chemistry. Plain and simple," he told the dog.

Rosie just pressed her head further into his hand. With distance between them, Robert decided he was over thinking it – they didn't even know each other for fuck's sake. It was sexual tension. Nothing more, and nothing less.

He wasn't sure if he believed that, but he knew he couldn't live with himself if he pursued anything with Sophie. She was out-of-bounds and he needed to remember that.

CHAPTER 6

They spent the next few days consciously avoiding each other, while pretending a casualness that Sophie was pretty sure neither felt. Whenever she thought of that moment in the bedroom, which was often, her cheeks grew warm and her chest tightened.

She was torn between guilt and desire, which were compounded by her being out of her comfort zone and not having Sara to talk things over with.

She distracted herself by setting up her laptop at the kitchen table and trawling through job websites, immersing herself in the prospect of a fresh start. The police had called with an update, saying they'd yet to make contact with Damien but that for the time being she was safer where she was.

Which was well and good for them, they weren't on high alert waiting for a frog to jump on their bum.

Settling back to her laptop after one such fraught trip to the bathroom, she received the welcome ping of an incoming email. Internet service out here was sketchy and frustrating as hell.

Hastily clicking on her inbox her heart lifted when she saw it was from Sara. Her glow of happiness was tinged with wistfulness – for all that she relished the peace and quiet out here, she missed her best friend. This self-imposed exile, while necessary, was lonely.

Sara had been true to her word, and had packed Sophie's

belongings and placed them in storage, saying she'd called in a favour and the cost was negligible. Sophie shook her head and heaved a sigh. As well-connected as Sara was, she knew well and good those connections were in Sydney's high society – and not likely to revolve around removalists or storage facilities.

As grateful as she was, it was frustrating to have to rely on other people, and something Sophie wasn't used to doing. As she ruminated on her faltering independence, another email pinged, also from Sara.

From: sara.morrison@highgloss.com.au
To: sophie.richards@gmail.com

Hey lovely! Hope you're coping out there in the sticks. Sneaking out of the office for a coffee is no fun without you. I talked to a couple of the guys in the art department for Health & Fitness mag and they're going to flick through some freelance work if you're keen? Call me soon, and say hi to the cowboy. Missing your face. Much love, Sara PS. You left your Prada sunglasses behind... they look better on me anyway xx

Sara had been looking for an opportunity to swipe those sunglasses. And it's not like Sophie was going to miss them – she was pretty sure the paddocks of cattle weren't going to appreciate designer accessories.

She started as the screen door to the verandah banged and Robert's boots thunked to the floor as he removed them.

Knowing he was about to enter the kitchen, Sophie's heart rate picked up and she resisted the urge to run her hands through her hair. Her excitement was because she was bored and lonely, not because she liked him. At least, not in *that* way. So it shouldn't matter if her hair was messy.

Even so, seemingly of its own volition a hand quickly tucked a loose strand behind her ear. Traitorous body.

The spacious kitchen had been renovated fairly recently but the large room appeared to shrink as Robert's bulk filled the doorway. Dear god the man was big. His energy and vitality sucked all the oxygen from the room, and Sophie let out a small gasp.

Her mind may have decided she didn't like him in that way, but her body had clearly missed the memo because it was acting like a hussy.

An achy heaviness settled between her legs, causing her to squirm in the kitchen chair, and her nipples tightened into deliciously painful nubs. Crossing her arms over her chest to hide them only caused a tingle at the contact, and she shamelessly pressed against them harder until she caught herself and dropped her arms quickly.

She needed to get a hold of herself.

Apparently unaware of the fevered reaction his presence had caused, Robert greeted her and headed straight for the coffee machine.

"God I need caffeine, this afternoon has been one clusterfuck after another," he growled, reaching out a long arm to grab the milk from the fridge. "Do you want one?"

He still hadn't turned to look at her, and Sophie felt the frustration rolling off him. No wonder he hadn't noticed her reaction to his arrival, he had his own tension that was tightening the set of his shoulders and causing that low throaty tone in his voice.

"I'd love one, thanks." She rose from her chair and approached the island bench somewhat cautiously. "What happened?" she wasn't sure he wanted her involved in his problems, however much he was caught up in hers. And even though her knowledge of the farming world outside this house was non-existent, she wanted to help.

Tapping the aromatic beans he'd just ground into the machine, he flipped a switch and turned around, crossing heavy arms across his chest as he leaned back onto the counter and faced her.

"I called the bank manager and got into an argument with her. Apparently without my brother's signature I can't change access to the farm's bank accounts, which is what I was trying to do to stop him bleeding me dry."

Sophie's skin prickled uncomfortably at the sharp way Robert eyed her as he said this. Surely he didn't think she had anything to do with Damien withdrawing funds from the farm? She hadn't even known her ex had a financial involvement in the property.

"And I was so pissed off when I hung up that I dropped my phone into the auger I was using to move some feed grain, and now the bloody thing is useless." Robert shook his head angrily and then sighed, shoving his hands through already mussed hair. "Sorry, it's not your fault."

He turned back to the coffee machine.

"Is it a silly question to ask what an auger is?"

Letting out a heavy breath he turned to look at her again, this time with a small smile. "Not a silly question, city girl. It's a screw elevator in a long metal tube that's used to raise and transport grain into trucks or grain bins. And mobile phones don't fare so well when they get dropped in."

"That sucks, sorry."

Turning again, he finished making their coffees and handed her a mug.

"It does suck. I wanted to touch base with the police, so I've come back to use the landline. Have you heard any news?"

Leaning with her butt against the island counter was surprisingly comfortable, and Sophie settled into the conversation with Robert, who was similarly positioned against the opposite bench.

As she relayed what little news the police officer had imparted, she noticed Robert's eyes roving over her body. He might have apologised for seeing her half-dressed, but she was pretty damn sure he didn't regret it.

"Are you concerned about his safety?" Robert interrupted her thoughts.

"No. Are you?"

"If it's one thing Damien is good at, it's looking out for himself. He's going to lay low until he can get enough money out of the farm to pay off the loan shark," Robert muttered.

"Do you think he knows the police are involved?"

"Probably not. But it's safer that they are. Better to end up in jail than at the bottom of Sydney Harbour with his feet in cement."

"In jail?!" For the first time, Sophie felt real fear for Damien. She knew he was in trouble, but she'd never doubted he'd come out the other end unscathed and perfectly unruffled. That was just the way Damien was.

"You heard the police in Sydney. I'm pretty sure he's under investigation for possible insider trading. If that sticks, it's jail time for sure."

They looked at each other without speaking.

With no warning he was standing in front of her, crowding her back against the kitchen bench. Maintaining eye contact he lifted a finger and swiped it across her top lip, before sucking the froth he'd captured into his own mouth.

Sophie watched his lips close around his finger and stopped breathing. Still looking into her eyes, he gently removed the coffee mug from her grasp and set it on the counter before moving closer still. Their bodies were flush against each other and Sophie had to tilt her head back to see his face.

"I shouldn't do this, but I don't think I could stop if I tried." And he cupped the back of her head in a large hand, caging her against the bench as he propped his other hand against it and leant down.

Sophie's eyelashes fluttered closed and all thought fled as his sensuous lips descended. All she could do was feel, melting into him as he slanted firm lips over hers and softly, softly demanded entry.

Opening her lips on a breathy sigh she was overwhelmed by sensory heaven; he tasted of rich coffee and his velvety tongue stroked hers, dipping even deeper as he moved his knee between her legs and pressed against her – inflaming a need that instantly became a burning inferno inside her.

Her hands twisted into in his hair, holding on and pushing down. She wanted *more*. This was insane. This was heaven. And she didn't ever want to stop.

———

Robert hadn't meant to kiss her. He hadn't even thought

about it. His body craved contact with hers and before he knew it he was drowning in her.

A kitten-like mewl sounded from her and brought him to his senses. Raising his head he set his hands on her shoulders and took a step back – her lust-dazed eyes following him.

And then she licked her lips, and he couldn't stop himself. He dove right back in and claimed those full, lush lips. While the first kiss had been slow and measured, as he'd explored the nirvana of her mouth, now he was frantic and she was just as eager, moving her hands to his lower back, kneading and holding him closer.

He wanted more. He wanted everything. He wanted to lick every single of inch of her silky skin as she moaned his name. He wanted to sink himself so deep inside her that his world would never be the same. The woman had gotten under his skin and made him lose control and damn if he didn't need it.

"Okay, stop. I need to breathe." She fisted her hands and held them against his chest, not raising her eyes to meet his. His heart hammered in his chest and he could see the pulse jumping under the delicate skin of her throat, her uneven breath betraying just how affected she was.

"This is –" She couldn't finish the sentence. In her silence, he removed his knee from the warmth between her legs and released his hold on her glossy hair, which had tumbled down around her shoulders.

"Crazy, I know." He took a step back, putting some distance between them even as his body screamed for him to hoist her up and wrap her legs around his waist.

Crazy on so many levels. He just didn't know whether to trust his gut feelings on her having no ulterior motives, or question whether his lust was clouding her true intentions.

How could she not have known about Damien's financial strife and his plan to sell the farm to solve the problem?

Because they've been broken up for six months?

Okay, there was a chance she didn't know about Damien's scheming. But that didn't change the fact that she was his *brother's* ex-fiancé. That was just a cut and dried no-go zone. Right?

His cock was disagreeing. Strongly.

Time to remove himself from this situation, before things escalated any more than they had already. He had no intention of ceding any of his high moral ground to Damien, which would absolutely happen if he let anything further happen with his ex *almost*-sister-in-law.

He took another step back, and still her darkened eyes held his, as though waiting for his next move. The perceptible rise and fall of her chest and lushly parted lips indicated that, crazy or not, she was more than ready to see where this could lead.

Christ, who the hell came up with that old adage 'two wrongs don't make a right'? Because he'd *really* like to use Damien's wrongs as an excuse to take this further with Sophie. And he was damn sure it would feel right.

"Robert?" her soft voice focused him.

They couldn't do this.

"I'm going. I just – yeah, uh, I'm going." He sounded like a tongue-tied teenager. Grimacing at his own awkwardness he backed out of the kitchen and headed straight for the study. Unchanged since his father had used it, the study was the hub of the farm – where records were meticulously kept, finances managed and strategies developed.

Sinking heavily into the desk chair he scrubbed his hands

over his face, taking a moment to compose himself. That had been intense, and his body was thrumming with need. Linking his hands behind his head he leaned back in the chair, concentrating on the ceiling in an attempt to focus.

That had been one hell of a kiss.

It was another five minutes before he made a call to organise a replacement mobile phone to be sent out and, after noting in the farm diary which cattle had been moved and to which paddocks, he mentally calculated how many days they'd now been without rainfall. Logging onto the Bureau of Meteorology's website gave no hope for any in the near future. He was just lucky that water allocation for irrigation hadn't been cut back yet.

The farm was in a better financial position than most, even with Damien owning half the property and Robert paying him an above-market lease to farm it. Even so, it just wasn't financially viable for him to buy Damien out. And if Damien went ahead with selling his half of the farm, it would drastically cut Robert's operations and severely affect his income.

Not to mention land that had been in his family for generations would be lost. Not happening on his watch.

Picking up the phone he dialed the number for his solicitor, swallowing impatience when Martin Lawrence was unavailable. It wasn't the secretary's fault that his life was going to hell in a hand basket.

In a strained voice, he left a message asking if there had been any further word from the stock and station agent that Damien had employed to facilitate the sale. And then he tried Damien's phone number again. Just like all previous attempts, it rang straight to voice mail.

He just wished his little brother would *talk* to him. There
had to be a way of sorting this out, without having to resort
to selling half the farm.

There just had to be.

CHAPTER 7

Sophie spent the next day in a daze. Unable to think of anything but that incendiary kiss with Robert.

She had lived totally in that moment when his lips were locked with hers and their bodies were pressed so intimately together. The desire that had urged her on had obliterated any thoughts – the only thing that had mattered was the pure physical feeling. And she'd never felt like that before.

It scared her – to have been so lost in the moment that she'd forgotten herself.

Her life was one big mess at the moment, and complicating that by starting something with Damien's brother was definitely not the smart thing to do.

She was only planning on being here a few more days, a week at the most. And after that, she needed to get her life back on track, walking away from her past with Damien for good. And that included Robert.

It had been six months since she'd broken off the engagement, it was time to start fresh. New job. New home. New life. She had to stop letting her past get in the way of her moving forward – no more dwelling on what could have been.

Even before she'd walked away, her relationship with Damien had been struggling for a long time, and with a wedding on the agenda she'd struggled to salvage *something* they could move forward with. But there had come a point when she had to acknowledge there was nothing left of the man she'd fallen in love with. Who Damien had become was a stranger she didn't like.

She'd been angry with Damien, so angry, that he'd given up on her. On their life together. And it had been a pretty fabulous life. Sophie had felt like she belonged with Damien; on his arm people accepted her, she was invited places, she was known. For someone who had always felt like she hadn't belonged, that was a heady thing and no small part of the attraction.

Had she loved being a couple with him more than she'd actually loved the man? Had it been so wrong to want to be wanted?

In her heart Sophie knew that she'd worked harder than she should have had to, to make their relationship work. Would she rather have stayed in on a Wednesday night to read a book with a cup of tea? Probably, but as Damien's fiancé she had been known as the fun, party-ready chick, so weekday nights were usually just as hectic as the weekend.

This whirlwind of society meant she rarely spent time with Damien when they weren't 'on' – hosting dinners, attending parties, being seen where it counted. She didn't think they'd ever just sat at their own kitchen table eating breakfast and quietly reading the newspaper together.

So it almost felt like she was leading a parallel life here with Robert, because it was the quiet, every day tasks they were living with each other. Albeit tentatively, as they each skirted the issue of their undeniable physical attraction.

Last night Robert had left for a Rural Fire Service meeting and hadn't come home until after Sophie had gone to bed, and he'd been up and gone at daybreak this morning, leaving a short note explaining he'd packed a lunch box and wouldn't return until dark.

They'd fallen into a pattern of only seeing each other of an evening, when they sat down to eat a meal Sophie had prepared. Her culinary skills were limited, and she knew her meal repertoire was going to be exhausted very soon. But she felt strongly she needed to contribute in some way, and so had spent the afternoon on a culinary website coming up with meal options. Between Robert's well-stocked pantry, the deep freeze and the vegetable garden, she had an impressive selection of ingredients.

Tonight's meal of chicken, leek and mushroom pie was actually easier than she'd thought to make, and tasted pretty damn good.

"You look pleased with yourself," Robert commented, as he tucked into his pie with gusto. "This is great."

"I know, right? I love baking, but I've never really cooked before, and I wasn't sure how this would turn out."

By unspoken agreement, it appeared they were both going to avoid mention of the kiss, and Sophie wasn't sure how she felt about that. Her head was relieved. Her body? That treacherous hussy was panting for more.

Just then the lights flicked, dimmed, and went out. Because of the longer daylight hours of Daylight Savings they weren't plunged into darkness, but the cutting off of the air-conditioner was going to be noticed quickly.

"Damn. I'd forgotten about the enforced blackout. They're doing maintenance on the electricity lines and we'll be without power for the next 12 hours."

They stared at each other over their half-eaten meal. Usually after dinner they each sat on their laptops, he catching up on farm bookwork and she tinkering on her graphic design portfolio. It was companionable and easy and occasionally they'd flick the television on for some background noise.

With her laptop's battery needing a boost and no light to work by anyway, Sophie realised she was at a loss of how to fill the evening hours.

She would *not* think about things she could do with Robert to fill that time, even though she ached to run the pad of her thumb over the stubble on his face and the pulsing between her legs remembered very well the delicious feel of his thigh wedged there.

Sexual intimacy with Damien had been stale for longer than Sophie was willing to admit, even before they broke up. Her body had been without so long that now it was responding greedily.

To the wrong man.

———

"No electricity? Does this happen often?" Sophie looked concerned, and Robert realised she didn't know this was a common occurrence when living in the bush.

"We had a big electrical storm last week that took out some power lines, so I guess that's what they're working on. Listen, why don't we take this out to the front verandah, there should be a cool breeze out there now."

He grabbed a bottle of cabernet sauvignon and two glasses on his way out, hoping that alcohol would dull his sharp awareness of *every little thing* the woman did.

She was under his skin and he was hyper aware of her

every action. The way she smelled. They way she tilted her head to the side as she listened. He liked the way she didn't feel the need to fill a silence with chatter.

He'd noticed she'd started to weed the front garden bed, and it interested him she didn't seem to mind getting dirt under her fingernails. And he'd watched her befriend the mean old farm cat, which only ever hissed at him. When his housecleaner, Mrs Maloney, had come over yesterday, Sophie had insisted on helping her.

As his brother's fiancé, he'd pegged her as a shallow, self-centered socialite. It was actually annoying to find out she was nothing like this, because he'd really appreciate a couple of reasons to *not* like her.

He was resolved there wasn't going to be a repeat the mistake of kissing her – but with it replaying over and over in his head, his body was telling his head where it could stick its resolutions.

They finished their meal in comfortable silence, before a flock of galahs alighted in a nearby gum tree, screeching loudly.

"I thought I'd really struggle with living so far away from the city, but it's so peaceful out here. Well, apart from the galahs."

"You haven't felt lonely? Missed the bright lights?"

"Funnily enough, not that much. I didn't realise how much I needed I break from all that I guess. I miss Sara, and some of the other girls on the magazine, but I'm in contact with a few of them with this new freelance thing, so that's been good."

"I didn't realise you were working again," said Robert, stacking their empty plates and re-filing their wine glasses.

"Is that what you've been doing on your laptop?"

"What did you think I was doing? Trawling Tinder and stalking people on Facebook?" She laughed; "I have to do something to get some cash flowing again. I really only started the freelance gig yesterday, but I registered for an ABN and I've playing around with a business logo for a while."

"So what kind of work are you doing?" he was genuinely interested, noting with enjoyment the way her eyes lit up.

"One of the health and wellness titles in my old magazine's publishing house is on deadline and has outsourced some of their photo editing to me – which has kept me pretty busy. I love working with photographs, I guess I'm a bit of an amateur photographer."

Robert raised his eyebrows in respect and stretched his legs out. "I didn't know you were into photography as well as graphic design. I'm part of a beef producer's collective that has brought a PR company onboard, and they've been hounding us to sort out our branding. Maybe we could employ you?"

"Seriously? That would be amazing. But you really should look at some of my work before you make a decision and," she added cheekily, "You don't even know if you can afford me. I could be *very* expensive."

"Of that I have no doubt," he responded drily, "But I'm sure you'd be worth it."

She licked those delicious lips of hers and didn't say a word, just drained her wine without breaking eye contact. The loaded moment was broken by the farm cat's approach, who looked disdainfully at Robert and then wound itself around Sophie's legs.

"I've fed that thing since it was a kitten, and this is the

thanks I get."

Sophie leant down to scratch behind the feline's ears, exposing just a hint of creamy cleavage. Oh Jesus he was in trouble.

He stood abruptly. "I'm going to take these plates inside. Why don't I grab some candles and Monopoly and we can have a game?"

She grinned at him and clapped her hands. "I haven't played Monopoly in years! But I should warn you, I don't lose."

"We'll see."

They'd played for over two hours, and Robert didn't know when he'd last had such a good time. They'd laughed together and sworn at each other. Cheated recklessly and taken chances with abandon. In the end they were both bankrupt and Sophie was hiding her yawns.

"Time to hit the hay, I'm up early in the morning. You can come with me, if you're serious about getting some photos to pitch to the collective?" He pushed out his breath on a huff when he realised he'd been holding it, waiting on her answer.

"Definitely. I'd love that," the response was gratifyingly eager. "Early morning light is perfect for photography, and I can use those photos to put together a proposal for branding and marketing."

She paused in her packing up of the board game and tilted her head slightly to the side. "It's funny, before coming out here I didn't ever wonder about the food I bought in the supermarket, or ordered in a restaurant. I didn't think about where it had come from, or the people who produced it." Standing up, she reached for his empty wine glass and avoided eye contact. "I bet you grow really excellent beef," she said, almost shyly.

"You can bet your ass I do."

She finally raised her head to catch his eye and they both laughed, moving companionably inside.

"Sweet dreams then." He left her at the door of her bedroom, forcing his feet to keep on moving.

My brother's girl. My brother's girl.

CHAPTER 8

The morning sun was tentatively appearing over the paddock's horizon, the wheat shimmering a soft pink in its glow. This early in the day the temperature was almost cool, and Sophie was glad she'd thrown a long sleeved t-shirt over her singlet.

The air was still, amplifying the sounds of the farm waking up as she and Robert made their way to the stables. They were met by soft, snuffling whickers from the horses who crowded each other at the fence stretching out their necks in greeting.

"I don't get a chance to ride them as much as I should, the motorbike is so much faster when you need to get things done. But we've always had horses on the farm and I don't want to give them up."

"I haven't ridden since I was about 10, but I'm pretty sure I remember the basics. I'm looking forward to getting back in the saddle."

Sophie realised she really *was* looking forward to exploring Robert's world on horseback, the romance of riding through the countryside would make for the kind of evocative photos she was hoping to capture.

Once saddled up Robert moved behind her and placed his large hands on her waist. Startled, she gave a little jump and spun around, which put her smack up against his very delicious smelling chest.

"Um, what are you doing?"

There was that smirk again. "I thought you might need a leg up."

"Oh. Right. No, I can mount by myself, but I might need you pass up my camera, if that's okay?"

"Sure, no probs." But he didn't move back, instead leaving his hands resting lightly on her, his hat tipped back on his head so he could look down at her.

"What is it about you Sophie, that's driving me so crazy?"

"I didn't know I was driving you crazy…"

"Madly. Completely. But I know I can't have you. Maybe that's what it is, wanting what I can't have."

Sophie's stomach swooped. In excitement and a whole lot of nervousness. Were they really going to discuss this now? They'd done such a good job of ignoring the physical awareness between them.

Before she could respond he'd stepped back, removing the warmth of his hands and pulling his hat back down on his head.

"Don't worry. Let's move out, before the sun gets too much higher. I want to show you our bulls, and some of the heifers have been early calving, so you should be able to get some good shots of the calves."

Sophie missed the heat of his nearness, and for a moment couldn't think of a thing to say. And then she remembered the camera slung around her neck, and the reason she was out here in the first place. Time to prove she could be professional, and get some amazing photos that could secure her the branding contract for the collective.

"Can I just get a few shots of you with the horse? I think the angle we need to take is the people behind the product

– personalize the farming lifestyle and get an emotional reaction from the buyer."

"Sure, I'll humor you, but the focus is on selling beef into the restaurant industry, not on me."

As Sophie adjusted the aperture on her camera she smiled to herself. If this handsome, rugged farmer with his beat up boots and sexy smile couldn't convince someone to buy beef, then she'd eat his hat.

As focused as Sophie was on the task ahead of her, she couldn't help but feel consumed by the man beside her. Robert's earthy, masculine scent was the base note on which balanced the dry smell of the dust and the sweet tang of the eucalypt trees.

His deep timbered voice was animated as he guided her over his land, telling her its history, showing his love of these wide open spaces. Clicking off shot after shot, Sophie was absorbed in capturing the essence of the landscape and the livestock, and the man who loved it.

She barely noticed the passing of time until a tiny trickle of sweat that ran down her back and Robert lead their horses under the shade of a tree.

"That sun is really starting to get some sting to it. What time is it? I feel like we've been out here forever, but for no time at all."

"A couple of hours. Let's have a quick drink and then head back to the stables. We can swap the horses for the jeep and head over to the old shearing shed. We don't run sheep anymore so it's falling down, but it should be a good backdrop for those photos you want to get of me with the dog."

Robert passed her a canteen of water, but as parched as she was, Sophie paused before taking a sip, watching as he tipped water on his hands to wash them off, captivated by his powerful throat muscles as he gulped his own water. She wanted to lick that throat. She wanted to bite him. She wanted…

Oh god, what am I thinking?

The problem was, she wasn't thinking. She was reacting, feeling, *wanting*.

"Not happy with that plan?" He was watching her and she realised she'd been staring at him. Luckily the staring hadn't been accompanied by drooling. *Just.*

"No, no. That sounds great. I really like the idea of using the textured wood of the shearing shed."

"But? There's a but there."

Sophie glanced down at her hands, loosely holding the reins of the bridle and fiddling with the horse's mane. She felt like she was going to burst with the tension between the two of them. They'd been dancing around this attraction to each other and her heart was feeling too big for her chest. It felt like she was going to have a heart attack when he got too close sometimes.

Surely it wasn't healthy for her heart to beat this crazily?

"What's happening between us?" she burst out, staring at him hotly. "I mean, we kissed and we shouldn't have, because I have a past with your brother. And I'm leaving soon. But I think I'm going crazy because I can't stop thinking about it. There's this *thing* between us…"

She dropped her eyes and trailed off, not able to raise her eyes to meet Robert's. Did she want this to happen? Could she live with herself if it *didn't*?

Her life had already been turned upside down, what was the harm in going all in and seeing what could happen?

"You're not the only one going crazy Sophie. I shouldn't have reacted to you like I did. Like I do. I'm feeling what you're feeling." His eyes looked steady and true back at her, giving her courage to stay the course.

"Really? Because I feel like I'm going to throw up." She lifted a small, anxious grin to him, her chest exploding with the beat of her heart.

He slid from his horse before tugging her from hers, their bodies coming together in a soft rush. Her skin tight with anticipation, she watched as he turned to loop their reins over a branch, before gently pushing her back against the tree trunk. He stood looking down at her, arms braced against the tree either side of her.

"Really."

———

"I think you're amazing Sophie. I've never known anyone like you." Robert lowered his forehead until it was touching hers, his eyes closed, his breathing strained. "I've tried so hard to ignore it, not just because Damien is my brother but because you and I, we're so different."

Defying his words Robert inhaled her sweet vanilla scent, lowering his mouth to kiss slowly down her neck and then back up, pausing at the tender spot behind her ear. She shivered, her back arching, her head falling against the tree.

"We're from different worlds. I want to find someone to share my life with, and you're not going to be here much longer. Whatever this is, there's no future for us together. But I just can't help myself," he groaned.

He had to know if the taste of her was as good as he remembered, and removing his hands from the trunk he cradled her head, guiding his mouth to hers, gently nipping at her lips until she granted access.

"You're going to be the death of me," he growled, before plundering her with is tongue, urgent and hard. She met him stroke for stroke, their mouths moving together with an intimacy that left him reeling.

"I've never – this is – I can't believe I feel like this over, just, a kiss," Sophie panted, removing her hands from where they were bunched in his shirt and holding her palms to her pink cheeks.

Not bothering to answer, Robert claimed her mouth again, thrusting his tongue the way he'd love to be thrusting his cock into the slick warmth between her legs. He slid his hand beneath her singlet to caress the fullness of her breast through the lace of her bra, her nipple instantly pebbling as his thumb and finger rolled it.

She broke the kiss on a gasp. "More Robert. I need more."

He didn't need urging. He wanted to give her so much pleasure she came undone. He wanted her crying out his name as he rocked her world.

Pushing up her singlet he dropped his head to suck at her nipple through the lace, while his large hand palmed the other breast. Impatient, he tugged the bra cups down so her creamy cleavage spilled out, dusky pink nipples pert and straining. He took one in his mouth, tongue circling and flicking while his fingers kneaded the other.

Sophie's hands clutched his head, fisting in his hair as she sighed and whimpered her pleasure. His own desire ratcheted up.

"Are you ready for this baby?" he asked hoarsely, slipping his hands down to unbutton her jeans.

Without waiting for an answer he slid down her quivering body, pushing her jeans off as he went. Kneeling in front of her he took a moment to appreciate the fine detailing of her lacy underwear before tugging at her boots and pulling the denim the rest of the way free.

Smoothing his hands back up her deliciously bare legs, he leant forward to cover her heat with his mouth, moaning into the fabric. He inhaled. God…he'd never known anything sweeter. If he didn't taste her *fast* he was going to lose his mind.

Her knees started to buckle as he slipped her panties down and placed one of her legs over his shoulder.

"Oh god, you're so ready for me."

He spread his knees further apart in the dirt to give more leverage, every muscle in his torso tight and primed. With single-minded determination he locked eyes with Sophie and slowly, purposefully, placed his mouth over her, sliding his tongue to find the tight nub of her clit. Sophie bucked against his face and used the hands that were still tight in his hair to push close, closer. He closed his eyes and sucked harder. He flicked his tongue exactly as he had earlier on her nipples and she cried out.

"I don't know if I can take much more Rob. Please," she begged.

He looked up from between her legs, seeing her breasts pushed up and over her bra cups, her head thrown back in abandon. She was so damn gorgeous. He was going to come in his jeans like a teenager if he didn't get some control real quick.

His tongue started a slow thrust inside her heat and he inserted a finger while his thumb kept a steady, relentless pressure on her nub. He could sense she was getting closer and slowed the pace, teasing her out.

"Robert!" She squeezed her legs tighter around his head and gripped ever harder into his hair. He loved knowing he had the power to make her utter those breathy, passionate cries. He felt like he could kneel here forever, lapping her sweetness. But her legs were weakening and it was time to bring her undone and let her fly.

His light, feathery tongue strokes plunged once more, his finger increasing its rhythm. When he slipped another finger in she moaned, "God, now, please. Robert I can't hold on much longer."

"Come for me baby."

He increased the tempo and renewed his assault on her oh-so-sensitive clit and was rewarded with her cry of release as she convulsed around him. He grinned into her wetness, relentlessly tonguing her until she was spent.

He took one last, slow lick before sitting back on his heels, raising his eyebrows playfully; "still feeling nauseous?"

CHAPTER 9

Sophie couldn't stop blushing as they rode their horses back to the stables. Her body was still thrumming with pleasure and the steady gait of her horse only compounded the shivery deliciousness of it.

She couldn't believe she'd lost control so completely. Up against a tree in the middle of a paddock!

Robert kept catching her eye and grinning, appearing very self-satisfied after his masterful performance. And it had been masterful. Sophie had never had her body played that way before. Her insides were all melty and quivery and her heartbeat *still* hadn't returned to normal. She wondered if it ever would when she was around him.

"So, that was uh, you know," she couldn't find the exact words.

"Incredible? Yeah, I know."

"You don't have to be so cocky about it."

"Well it was. Incredible. Seriously, I've never been so turned on by a woman, and you didn't even touch me," he drawled, leaning across his saddle and running a thumb over her swollen bottom lip.

"So, this – thing – we're doing…"

"You mean me giving you the best orgasm of your life?"

"Seriously," she looked at him. "I think we need to define what we're doing, exactly."

"Right, because you're not going to be here for much

longer, I know. But yesterday the cops said at least another week, and I don't want you going back to Sydney until it's absolutely safe. Fuck Sophie, it makes me wild to think about what could have happened to you."

Sophie shivered at the force behind Robert's words. Had Damien ever felt this strongly about her? He sure as hell had never given her an orgasm that explosive.

"Okay. But being here, it's just a temporary thing until I find my feet. It can be anything but love. Don't get me wrong, it's amazing being here with you, but this isn't my world. This isn't my forever."

"I'm not looking for forever with you, so this could be kind of perfect."

"So long as we're both clear. Anything *but* love."

"Anything but love," he agreed with a smile.

His gaze turned serious and he turned in the saddle to face her "I need to know, did you really have no idea about Damien taking money out of the farm's accounts and approaching our solicitor to organise the sale of half the property?"

Sophie flinched. Did he really think she could be so underhanded and outright *mean*? Granted, they hadn't known each other that long, but it hurt to think he could think so little of her.

"Robert, I didn't even realise what was happening right in front of me. Back when we were together some of my jewellery went missing, and he said he'd taken it to the jewelers to get cleaned, and then one of my credit cards bounced, but I'm not always great at keeping track of my finances… I'd been trying to organise with him to come into the bank to close our joint account and it wasn't until the real estate agent turned up saying my rent hadn't been paid in months that I checked it and found it empty. I had no idea. None."

"Okay, I believe you. I guess I just had to hear you say it," he sighed. "I have to call the solicitor back and see what my next move is. I don't know where I stand legally with this and it's difficult to know what to do when I can't contact Damien." They reined up at the stables and dismounted, "But this – us – I know exactly what my next move is," he smirked. "Get your cute butt up to the house while I unsaddle the horses. I'll be there in five minutes."

The silly grin Sophie had plastered on her face slipped when she climbed the verandah steps and found a pin-up girl languishing on the swinging cane chair.

She had blonde curls tumbling around her shoulders, breasts pushing up out of a too-tight shirt and snug jeans hugging long legs.

She appeared to be expecting Sophie, and narrowed her eyes speculatively as she sat straighter.

"Is Robert here?" The direct question and lack of greeting or introduction pissed Sophie off.

Who does this woman think she is?

"He's down at the stables. I'm Sophie, and you are?"

"So, the grapevine had it right for a change," the woman pursed her lips thoughtfully. "The question, I think, is who are *you*?"

The woman was not following the rules of social etiquette and Sophie sure as hell didn't like the tone she'd used, but there was an implied ownership in her last words that had Sophie on the back foot.

Robert hadn't mentioned anything about another woman and Sophie's heart gave a squeeze. He knew all about her romantic history, but she had no idea about his.

What she *would* like to know, was who this woman was and why she was here. "Robert didn't mention we were having company…"

The blonde's eyes narrowed further and she flicked her gaze up and down Sophie's body before locking eyes with her.

"We? You're on awfully familiar terms with my *boyfriend*." She rose slowly from the swing, thrusting her shoulders back so that her impressive chest was front and center. "Honey, I'm not sure what you think you're doing here, but Robert is mine."

"Really?" Sophie didn't try to hide her skeptical tone. Robert hadn't once mentioned there was a girlfriend on the scene, and if this blonde really *was* his girlfriend, then she'd be confronting *him* about Sophie being here. Not, as Sophie suspected, sussing out the perceived competition.

"You're from the city, I get it. You're like a shiny new toy for him. But you don't belong out here. Robert and I have a lot of history, and our relationship is just starting to get serious. So I really think it would be best if you went back to where you came from." Her words had been slow and measured, and she'd moved purposefully into Sophie's personal space.

If she was trying to be intimidating, it was damn well working. Sophie hated direct confrontation and desperately wanted to back away, but that would mean stepping down onto the stairs and she was already at a height, and cleavage, disadvantage. Nuh uh, she was standing her ground.

Just then Rosie the kelpie bounded onto the verandah and

leapt enthusiastically into the blonde, licking her hand and giving small yaps of excitement. So the dog was familiar with her, and pretty damn happy to see her as well.

"Hi Rosie girl," she cooed, bending down to pat the excited dog. "You be sure to tell Robert that Cindy stopped by." And with that she sauntered off the verandah and back to her vehicle, which Sophie only just now noticed parked under one of the jacaranda trees.

Oh god. This was only meant to be a fun fling while she was hiding out from the drama in her life, not turn into a turf war over a man she suspected she may like a little too much. What was she getting herself into?

———

Robert couldn't get back to the house fast enough. He'd spent the last couple of days fantasising about Sophie and none of it had come close to how incredible they'd been together.

He didn't know if he'd ever been this hard before, and it was killing him; he needed her legs wrapping his waist, to know how her tightness felt around him as he lost himself in her.

"Soph?" he stood at the kitchen door and wondered where she would be waiting for him. Hopefully naked and spread open for him on his bed, but he was happy to work with whatever she wanted…

He couldn't believe how freeing it was to have given in to the strumming tension between them. There was still residual guilt about being with his brother's ex, but the pressure on his chest had dissipated. Damien had walked away from this woman – he didn't deserve her.

Sure, it wasn't a forever thing. And he *had* only just told Cindy that he wanted more than casual – he wanted to settle down. But the attraction between he and Sophie was undeniable, it was stronger than both of them combined.

It was easy to tell Cindy casual sex wasn't enough when the chemistry didn't burn so bright it was blinding; he could hold out for a proper relationship because he wasn't consumed by a need for her.

The only hitch was that when Sophie left, he may not be able to settle with Cindy. With anyone. Once you've tasted this kind of desire, could you ever go back from it?

He shook his head to dislodge those kinds of thoughts.

With the knowledge she'd definitely had no involvement in the plans to sell the farm, his whole outlook on life had lightened.

Ever since that first phone call from the solicitor following Damien's instructions to sell up his share of the farm Robert had felt like his control was slipping and he was powerless to change the outcome.

He needed to negotiate some possible options with Damien, but he needed Damien present to do that. In the interim he was in limbo and, for a man who liked to get in and get things done, he'd been struggling with the lack of control.

Just knowing that Sophie was on his side – and hopefully in his bed – made everything seem brighter. Easier to manage.

He stalked through the house and headed straight for his room, pausing only briefly when he discovered it empty. Turning on his heel he made his way to Sophie's room and stopped in confusion at the sight of the closed door.

Not exactly what he'd been expecting. He knocked and then waited, his body strung tight with expectation.

"Sophie? Are you in there? Can I come in?" Nothing. "Soph, you've got me worried. I'm coming in, okay?"

The door wasn't locked and he pushed it open warily, unsure what to expect. He'd thought they'd come back to the house to continue where they'd left off in the paddock, and now this? Was she regretting their intimacy?

Hell no, you are not retreating from this now.

"Sophie? What's going on honey?"

She was sitting on the side of the bed her hands hiding her face. In two strides he was at her side, pulling her into his embrace. "What's wrong? Are you hurt?"

It was the urgency in his tone that made her raise her head. "I'm fine, I'm just – confused. I came out here to get away from all the drama of my life, and now… I guess I just need a little space."

He stared down at her, at a loss. They'd just shared the most incredible experience together, and now she wanted space?

"We're moving so quick, and we barely even know each other. I just think we need to slow things down." She stepped away from him but kept her palms flat against his chest.

"I don't understand. I thought you enjoyed before, I thought we were on the same wavelength?"

"Enjoyed may be the biggest understatement of the year," she smiled at him, her cheeks tingeing pink. The smile slipped. "I just – look. We agreed this was a fling, an interlude in our lives. You don't owe me anything, but I'm not sure I can do this if we're not going to be exclusive."

Robert wasn't sure why his chest tightened at the reminder

this was just a fling. He knew this wasn't forever; she wasn't the kind of woman who would settle into the country lifestyle permanently.

So why does the idea of her moving on to someone else make me want to punch something?

"I can do exclusive. Exclusive is fine. Why do you think that would be a problem with me?" Robert hoped confusion was evident in his face, because he couldn't for the life of him work out where Sophie was going with this.

He'd thought the two of them were fairly in-sync and he'd loved how straightforward and easy she was – nothing like the girls and their games he'd dated in the past. He couldn't shake the feeling he was missing something.

"Cindy dropped over and said to say hi."

And there it was. "Right. Cindy." How to explain this?

"Cindy and I, we go back a long way. I've known her since primary school, we've always knocked around together. In the last year or so we've been seeing each other, casually. But I was ready to commit to a proper relationship and she wasn't, so I told her we had to end it."

"So you're in love with her?"

"No."

"But you want to be in a relationship with her?" Sophie's confused head tilt indicated how well he was explaining this.

"I'm ready to settle down and share my life with someone. I'm not in love with Cindy, but I thought we should give it a chance. We're compatible, we have the same outlook on life… I thought it could work."

"You *thought* it could work, or you *think* it could work?"

He paused to gather his thoughts. After discovering the explosive passion that existed between he and Sophie, he wasn't sure he could ever settle for anything less. But that was something he'd need to address in the future, not worry about right now when Sophie was in his arms.

"Whatever may happen in the future, right here and now, Cindy is *not* my girlfriend and you're the only one I'm thinking about."

Sophie looked at him dubiously and he had the ridiculous feeling that the future of this *thing* with Sophie, whatever it was, hinged on her next words.

Panic rose up and he had to restrain himself from crushing her to him.

She blinked those long black lashes at him and furrowed her brow in a way he found overwhelmingly adorable. She started to speak and then stopped, biting her lip.

"What can I do? What do I need to do to show you that Cindy isn't an issue? I can't even believe we're talking about her right now. Please Soph," he implored, giving in and reaching for her again, "Believe me when I tell you that Cindy is *nothing* to be worried about."

He held her tight against him, her head tucked under his chin. Stroking her hair down her back he threaded his fingers through the silky strands and murmured into the top of her head. "You're the one I want to be with."

She sighed and pulled back her head. "Okay. I guess I just over-reacted because she was – uh, feisty."

It was Robert's turn to mimic Sophie's earlier furrowed brow; Cindy was strong-minded and could be pretty direct, but he'd never have described her as feisty. What exactly had she said to Sophie?

He lost his train of thought as Sophie snuggled closer, wrapping her arms around his middle. "So, now that we've cleared up your availability, can we get back on track with what we're *meant* to be doing?"

He burst into relieved laughter. "I think I can manage that."

Dipping his head, he caught those delicious lips of hers in a deep, drugging kiss. His heart rate kicked up immediately. Pressing closer against her soft body he knew he could lose himself in a kiss like this…

"… you on channel Rob? Rob? Robert, you on channel?"

The two-way radio in the kitchen crackled to life, Robert dimly acknowledging it as Sophie's lips clung to his.

"Mate, I can't get you on your mobile. Are you on channel?"

"Fuck!" Robert dragged his mouth from Sophie, groaning as her tongue came out to swipe across her plump lower lip. "That's my farmhand. I've to check that everything is okay."

He slipped a hand beneath his belt to rearrange his straining erection and Sophie pouted at him prettily. "Just hold that thought, okay?" He begged her, striding from the room.

"I'm here Jono, what's happening?" he asked, picking up the radio handset and forcing his mind away from the temptation of Sophie's mouth.

"Mate we've got some issues with the irrigation pipes in the second lucerne paddock. I'm going to need you out here."

Fuck. "Righto. Give me ten."

"Over and out."

CHAPTER 10

It was decadent to be having a bubble bath in the middle of the afternoon, but when Robert had been called away to deal with malfunctioning irrigation pipes, Sophie had decided a soothing soak was exactly what she needed to get her head together – even if, conscious of the water situation, the tub was only half full.

She lifted a dripping toe from the bubbles and flicked the tap to get another surge of hot water and then dipped her head back into the tub to let the water slick her hair back. She sighed.

What the hell has gotten into me?

After the shattering climax she'd experienced with Robert, she was still a shivery mess, which is what she was blaming her heightened emotions on. She'd barely shed a tear when she'd left Damien, having instead pasted a smile on her face and attempted to keep her world spinning. But just a few days with Robert and that world was spinning off its axis.

She wasn't jealous of Cindy, it wasn't like she had any claim on Robert – this was just a fun interlude while she sorted out her shit.

But the encounter with the blonde had definitely rattled her. Which was crazy, because even if she did want something more with Robert – *which she didn't* – she wasn't a jealous person by nature. It had never bothered her when Sydney socialites had simpered at Damien and clung to his side.

She was a secure, confident woman who knew her man had wanted her.

Until he hadn't. And maybe that was it; when Damien had flat out refused to change in order to keep her, the sting of rejection had shaken her self-assurance a little.

Okay, a lot. And that Cindy was a piece of work, how did Robert not think she was feisty? She'd been downright intimidating with that catty attitude and trumped up cleavage.

Robert had been so sincere when he'd promised that Cindy meant nothing to him, and Sophie had to trust that he would honour their agreement to be exclusive, for as long as this lasted between them.

Absentmindedly Sophie ran her hands lightly over her stomach and when her skin tingled she paused. That had been one mind-blowing orgasm and she couldn't believe they weren't right this moment exploring the possibilities of the desire between them; entwined in each other, consuming each other.

If Cindy hadn't shown up when she did Sophie had no doubt that not even irrigation issues would have tempted Robert to leave the bedroom.

Experimentally Sophie drifted her hands over her soapy breasts and instantly felt an answering throb between her legs. Closing her eyes and imagining it was Robert's calloused hands on her body, she circled around her nipples and tugged gently, and then harder. A small moan left her lips. A girl didn't always need a man to meet her needs.

When Robert returned late that afternoon Sophie was sitting at the kitchen bench, absorbed in her laptop. Without taking her eyes from the screen she waved him over, "I downloaded the photos from this morning and I've started editing them, they're really good. Like, *really* good."

His lips quirked n amusement as he came to stand behind her, "if you do say so yourself."

"I know, right?" she tore her eyes from the screen to grin at him. "But I really didn't know I could take photos like this. They've turned out exactly how I was imagining it in my mind. Look at the sunlight in this shot and the way it's casting all these sexy shadows on your face."

"I'm not sure that photos of me being 'sexy' is what we're really looking for here." He pressed closer and Sophie could feel his washboard abs flush against her back. He smelled deliciously of sunlight and a natural male huskiness that was making her a little lightheaded.

Dear god this man was divine.

"I get what you mean though. The colours are so rich, it's almost like the photos could show how the landscape sounds and smells. Does that make sense or am I talking complete rubbish?" He brushed his hands lightly over her shoulders and dipped his head to inhale near her neck.

She watched him step away to pull a beer from the fridge; "Do you want one?" he threw over his shoulder.

"Did you just smell my neck?"

"What if I did? You're lucky I stopped at that. I feel like I could eat you." He walked back towards her with a predatory gleam in his eye. Sophie realised she was practically panting as she gazed at him. What was a girl supposed to say to *that?*

He placed a beer next to her laptop and, taking a long swallow from his own drink, came to stand behind her again, leaning over her shoulder so she completely lost all concentration.

"Okay, show me more of this sexy photography that's going to sell my beef into Australia's best restaurants."

But he stopped his joking as she flicked through the ones she'd edited so far, as immersed as she'd been when he'd arrived. Sophie felt a surge of pride. Her photos really were stunning, perfectly depicting the raw Australian bush in gorgeous, saturated colour; the many detail shots shown together portraying the raw beauty of the landscape.

"Your – composition? Is that the right word? The way you've framed the cattle – it makes them look, goddamn good!" he laughed. "Seriously Soph, these are incredible."

"So you think the collective will like them?" Sophie wasn't sure where this sudden shyness had come from, but she realised she really, really wanted this job. She liked being involved in Robert's world, and she loved that she'd created these images with him.

"I'm happy to hire you on the spot." He leant closer and nuzzled into her hair, running his chilled bottle of beer lightly down her back, causing her to shiver. "But we really shouldn't mix business and pleasure. So how about you back away from the laptop and walk to the bedroom, before I lift you over my shoulder and carry you there."

"Hold up cowboy, aren't we meant to be going to that barbeque tonight?" Sophie spun around on her stool and reached up to loop her hands behind Robert's neck, pulling his head down so she could bite slowly on his bottom lip. "And after leaving me to my own devices all afternoon, I kind of think you deserve to wait a little longer until you get me into your bed."

She sucked his lip into her mouth and fanned her hands

over his stubble-roughened cheeks. In seconds he'd hoisted her off the stool and had her butt on the counter and her legs wrapped firmly around his waist.

With his hands on her lower back he dragged her forward so the impressive bulge in his jeans thrust against her heated core.

Without thinking, she rubbed against him, the slow burn she'd been building all afternoon igniting instantly. Her hands dipped under his shirt and finally, *finally* she was running her hands over that glorious chest of his.

It was hard and unyielding, smooth with a smattering of hair. She twisted her fingers into it and pulled, dragging his mouth into a consuming kiss and then biting his lip again none too gently.

"The kitten has claws," Robert drawled, trailing kisses down her neck and taking a nip himself. "I like it."

"The kitten is going to get ready. We have a barbeque to go to." She disentangled herself and tamped down her body's reluctance to distance itself from Robert's heat. The sexual tension that was strung so taunt between them was a delicious agony and she wanted to string it out. String them out until they physically couldn't stand it any longer.

"Go take a cold shower cowboy."

———

The saucy little wench was teasing him. Robert couldn't stop grinning as he finished his second beer, waiting on the verandah while Sophie got ready. All afternoon he'd struggled to concentrate on the job at hand. He could still smell her on his fingers and taste her in his mouth. He wanted to finish what they'd started in the paddock.

Damn Cindy.

He couldn't understand why she'd shown up at his house – she'd made it clear she wasn't ready to commit, and it had been a couple of weeks since he'd even seen her.

Had she changed her mind? Even a week ago he'd have been keen to jump into a relationship with her. Now? Not so much. Hell, not at all. Meeting Sophie had blown him out of the water, and completely changed his expectations for what he wanted with a woman.

The friendship and companionship he had with Cindy, even coupled with the pretty good sex they'd had, couldn't compete with the crackling electricity he had with Sophie. And while it wasn't going to be a forever thing, it was sure as hell going to make him want more out of future relationships.

Knowing what awaited him at home had had him in a lather; his arousal had been almost unbearable and he'd even considered chancing an encounter with a snake and taking a quick dip in the irrigation channel to cool off.

The wait was definitely worth it, he conceded, as Sophie appeared in the doorway and put a hand on her cocked hip.

"Do I look okay?"

He wasn't sure where this city girl had gotten ahold of cowgirl boots but damn if she wasn't totally rocking them. Her long, long legs showcased a tiny denim skirt and there was a faint hint of lace beneath a simple white t-shirt.

Her honey blonde hair fell in waves down her back and her full, inviting lips were a glossy soft pink. Mascara highlighted thick lashes that should already have been illegal, she had only to bat them in his direction and he was hard.

"I don't know if I want other men seeing you when you're looking like that," he answered honestly. "But if we're doing this, get into the ute real quick before I decide we're not going anywhere."

Dusk was falling over the dam in Wilko's front paddock when Robert pulled up. Festoon lights lit up the gathering, which was already pumping. A couple of the guys were dive-bombing each other into the water and the smell of sizzling sausages filled the air.

"I like this music," Sophie commented, climbing down from the ute. She smoothed a hand down her tanned leg. His cock jumped. They weren't going to last more than an hour here, before he was dragging her back home.

"It's Eric Church. Damn woman, stop drawing attention to those legs. In fact, I've got an old rugby jersey in the back of the ute, why don't you put it on?"

He was only half joking. If anyone so much as looked at her sideways, he'd have trouble controlling his fists. He didn't stop to examine why he was feeling so possessive, he just knew Sophie was *his*. He snagged one of her hands in his and they walked towards a group sitting around the tailgate of a ute.

"Rob my man! I wasn't sure if you'd show. I know if I had the delectable Sophie in my house I wouldn't have left it!" Wilko winked at Robert as he cuffed him on the shoulder and made to move around him to hug Sophie.

"I told you before mate, hands off." His tone was gruff but he offset it with a smile, shoving Wilko good-naturedly out of the way. "Where's this party you promised me?"

Michelle Evans came up beside Wilko and wound her arms tightly around his waist; her eyes scanned Sophie up and down before she flashed a bright smile. "Hi darl! You must be Sophie, I'm Michelle. Come on over and I'll get you a rum, or are you a wine girl? You look like you might be a wine girl."

"You know what? Rum would be fantastic right now."

Robert watched the two walk over to the esky and hoped he'd made the right decision in bringing Sophie here. This was a long way from her world of champagne and glitter. Welcome to his world of rum and dust.

For the last half hour Robert had only half listened to the conversation around him, as he kept an eye on Sophie. She was chatting with Lani Mayberry who, for a married woman in her late thirties, still turned heads – even heavily pregnant and carting around her boisterous three-year old son. She was sweet as well and from the stories he'd heard, overnight she'd turned her husband from a wild man-about-town into the family man he was today.

"Robert, you better not be checking out my woman," it was Henry, Lani's husband. He raised his eyebrows playfully but there was a warning note of steel under the words. Just as Lani's beauty was well known, so too was Henry's almost obsessive protectiveness. The man would go caveman quicker than a brown snake if he thought he needed to, and he was one of the few men Robert knew who was built bigger than he was. No way was he going head to head with Henry Mayberry.

"Henry, good to see you. Trust me, I've only got eyes

for one woman."

That did not *sound like something you'd say about a fling.*

Whatever. In a crowd of red-blooded males Robert felt the need to claim what was his. Even if what was his was only going to be for a short while.

"I'm glad I ran into you, actually. I had an out of town real estate agent call me out of the blue, saying that a local property was about to come up for sale. He was on for the hard sell but wouldn't disclose the property's name, but from the size and location I could only think he was talking about Acacia Ridge. I didn't know you were looking to put it on the market." The older man watched him, knowing that something wasn't right, but unsure what that was.

Robert coughed forcefully and choked down the mouthful of beer he'd just swallowed.

What the hell?

"Did you get the name of the real estate agent? To be honest, I'm having some issues with my brother." Robert ran his hands through his hair and stifled the urge to break something. "I have no intention to sell, but he's making things fucking difficult at the moment."

At least with the name of a real estate agent he had a chance of tracking down Damien and finding out what his expectations were. There was no way in hell he was losing the family farm.

CHAPTER 11

Sophie was surprised at how much she was enjoying herself. She decided she really liked rum and may never go back to champagne again.

"Michelle can be hard work, but she means well," said Lani, as Michelle ducked away. "She's taking her hostess duties very seriously." An amused look played over Lani's beautiful features.

Working on a glossy magazine Sophie was forever surrounded by gorgeous women, but there was something about Lani that was captivating. Luckily, in addition to being stunning, she was also excellent company and had been giving Sophie a running commentary of all the partygoers.

"So tell me, the local grapevine has you pegged as Damien's ex-fiancé, but you've hardly taken your eyes off Robert since you got here. Where is this mysterious other brother who I've never met?"

It was the warmth of Lani's voice and her gently raised eyebrow that encouraged Sophie to answer.

"It's all a bit messy at the moment. Hell, it's a *lot* messy." She took a gulp of her rum and coke and her eyes once more strayed to where Robert was standing. A soft evening wind was ruffling the curling ends of his hair and he was animated and laughing. Sophie's insides quivered all over again.

"I left Damien six months ago, but since then he's taken off and left a massive mess behind," she sighed, thankful for

Lani's sympathetic expression. "I had to get out of Sydney and Robert brought me back here. I just needed some time to sort my life out, and then we, well – he's just so –."

Hot. Amazing. Driven. Did I mention hot?

"We kind of have this thing…" she trailed off.

"You could start a fire with the sparks flying between the two of you. He looks like he wants to throw you over his shoulder and carry you off into the night!" laughed Lani.

Sophie blushed, toes curling because this was exactly what he'd threatened to do earlier. "It's just awkward timing. I'm not going to be here for all that long and the last thing I should be doing is re-bounding with my ex-fiancé's *brother*. And I should be sorting out what I'm going to do with my life, not getting caught up in a romance that's not going anywhere…"

"If there's one thing I've learned, it's that you can't control what your heart wants," said Lani, slowly rubbing her pregnant belly and smiling across the crowd at a man Sophie presumed to be her husband.

"It's not my heart that's doing the wanting, trust me," Sophie corrected wryly.

She was grateful when Lani laughed and re-directed the conversation.

"So you were telling me about the photography you've done for the beef collective, do you do any other kind of photography? I'd love to get some family shots taken before this next bub arrives."

"Well I'm actually a graphic designer, not a photographer. But I have a terribly expensive camera that tends to take beautiful photos. I'd be happy to take some for you."

"That would be amazing! And stop being so modest. I've

got a top of the line camera and I can't take a good photo to save myself."

Sophie was ridiculously pleased to be asked, Lani was being so sweet and she was excited about the possibilities open to her if she were to pursue her passion for photography.

"Oh I almost forgot, we're heading away to the coast the day after tomorrow for a couple of weeks, and there may not be much time between when we get back and when this baby arrives. Would it be a massive imposition to ask if you could come over tomorrow to do the shoot?"

Sophie laughed at Lani's pleading look. "Let me consult my non-existent diary… oh look, I seem to have tomorrow free."

"Brilliant! What time suits?"

"The earlier the better, the morning light out here in the country is divine."

"Archie is up at 5am most mornings, so early isn't an issue. Any time after that works for us." She clapped her hands excitedly. "I know it's a bit silly, but I really feel like we've known each other for ages. We're going to be good friends, I just know it."

Making friends, as opposed to acquaintances, didn't always come easy to Sophie, and she was thrilled with the connection she felt with Lani. She'd been missing Sara like crazy and it felt good to know there was someone out here who 'got' her. Because while she felt a strong connection with Robert it was almost overwhelming and it was *definitely* confusing.

"Don't look now, but that's Cindy Haworth over there with Robert. I'd watch that one. She looks like butter wouldn't melt in her mouth, but I have a feeling she could be a handful.”

Not able to help herself, Sophie immediately glanced over at Robert. Cindy was draped all over him and it felt like a sucker punch. The blonde was overly animated as she participated in the group conversation, with a hand resting on Robert’s bicep.

Sophie didn’t realise she was holding her breath until Robert casually removed the hand. She exhaled loudly.

“I had the pleasure of meeting Cindy earlier this afternoon. She claimed Robert was her boyfriend.”

“I’m pretty sure she’s the one who didn’t want to be in a relationship, and I heard they’d cooled things off,” reassured Lani. “But I wouldn’t trust her as far as I could kick her. Get over there girl and claim your man.”

Gathering her courage and taking a gulp of rum, Sophie started towards Robert, purposefully ignoring the sly look Cindy shot her, as though daring Sophie to touch what was hers.

Lani was right, she may only have a short-term thing happening with Robert, but right here, right now, he was her man, and she sure as hell wasn’t going to let a small town girl with a catty tongue intimidate her.

———

They’d been here for over an hour, and Robert was ready to leave. Definitely not something his mates would understand, as he was legendary around these parts for partying until dawn.

But right now, the only partying he wanted to do was

between the sheets of his bed with a certain city girl.

He'd struggled to hold a conversation all evening because he couldn't keep his attention from wandering to her; current wheat prices and the pre-training program for the local rugby team just couldn't compete with the sight of her delicious ass in that tiny denim skirt and those smooth tanned legs that went on forever.

I want her on her back, with those legs thrown over my shoulders…

He was jerked back to the present by the arrival of Cindy, who stood just a little too close and placed an overly familiar hand on his arm. She was dripping in a musky perfume that was coming on too strong, making him long for the light vanilla scent he associated with Sophie. He hoped like hell this wasn't going to be awkward.

"Sophie told me you called around this afternoon, why didn't you stay for a beer?"

When he'd told her he couldn't continue with their mutually beneficial arrangement he'd stressed that he wanted to stay friends. And while he needed Cindy to know that Sophie was on the scene, he didn't want to completely blow her off. After all, they'd known each other a long time and he did consider her a friend. Just not one with benefits any more.

"Oh she's a darling, isn't she? How long is she staying for? I haven't seen Damien here."

Robert gritted his teeth. No one had mentioned Damien all evening, for which he'd been thankful. "Why would Damien be here? They broke up six months ago. Soph is with me."

God he loved the sound of that. His face broke into a smile when Sophie started to move towards them. He knew this was just a fling, and honestly that suited him just fine.

Honestly?

He mentally shook himself. He knew it took a certain kind of woman to be happy living on a relatively isolated farm. Sophie was many amazing things, but a small town girl wasn't one of them. A short-term relationship was all they could ever have, and right now that sounded pretty damn perfect.

"Hey babe, enjoying yourself?" Robert put more distance between himself and Cindy as he tucked Sophie against his side, his arm wrapping around her possessively.

"I am, Lani is so lovely." Sophie took a deep breath and then nodded a greeting to Cindy. Wow. He really hadn't pegged her as the jealous type, but she wasn't even going to say hello?

"Cindy was saying how great it was to meet you this afternoon."

The festoon lighting was good for ambiance but not so much for clarity, and Robert wasn't sure if Sophie's face had just gone a little red. But he did feel her stiffen against him. Was she still thinking there was something going on between he and Cindy?

"Oh it really was so great to meet you, we don't often get new people visiting town, especially not city slickers!" smiled Cindy. "You must be dying in this heat and dust. I bet you can't wait to get back to the bright lights."

"Not really. Robert is being an excellent host, if you know what I mean."

The cheeky minx winked up at him and then smiled sweetly at Cindy. Robert bit back a laugh. If she felt she needed to mark her territory, who was he to stop her? He was just relieved she was going to move past his history with Cindy.

"I know, isn't Robert just the best? So why did you leave Sydney? Have you been sick? Because you're awfully thin."

"Excuse me?"

Right, might be time to step in here. Before Robert could change the subject Cindy just kept on putting her high-heeled foot in her mouth.

"It's just so refreshing to meet someone who doesn't care how they look!"

Robert cringed, even though he was sure it was an inadvertent comment and Cindy hadn't intended to be insulting. She was probably feeling nervous around Sophie's sophistication.

And he guessed that from Cindy's point of view, her hot pink frilly dress was proving she cared about her presentation. From his point of view, Sophie's appeal was all under the clothes. She could be wearing a grain sack and still raise his temperature.

To Sophie's credit, she barely blinked. "Robert sweetie, let's go home."

Holding his arm and with her head held high, she waved goodbye to Lani and Michelle and led the way back to the vehicle.

"Don't get me wrong, I'm more than happy to be leaving right now. But I don't think Cindy meant to offend you." He leant down to nuzzle her ear, "let me take you home and show you how much I worship the way you look."

"So you only like me for my looks?" She spun on him as they reached his ute, a furious expression on her adorable face.

"Come on kitten, you can't have it both ways. Are you mad because Cindy doesn't think you look good, or mad because I do?" He chuckled and pushed her up against the side of the vehicle. "And trust me, I think you look very, *very* good."

He went back to her ear, nibbling and then trailing light kisses down her neck, his big hands stroking down her back until she relaxed into him. He cupped his hands over her denim-covered backside and squeezed her perfect cheeks, biting gently into her shoulder. "I need to get you home. Right. Now."

With her palms flat against his chest Sophie pushed him away and shot a glare over his shoulder. "She's watching us."

Before he could turn to where she was looking, her eyes snagged his and she gave him an impish grin, "May as well give her something to talk about."

She raised her arms and clasped her hands behind his neck, tugging him down so she could reach his lips, demanding and hungry. Her hands tangled in his hair and her legs straddled one of his – he thought he may combust when she started to rub her core provocatively against his jean-clad leg, and when she pulled his bottom lip into her mouth and sucked on it he let out a deep growl.

The kitten's claws were out again. He held her face in both his hands and claimed her mouth with his. She tasted sweetly of rum and there was nothing tentative about the way she met his tongue thrust for thrust. Her hands had slipped under his shirt and were scratching at his back, driving him to a madness of desire. He needed her closer, he wanted them joined.

Giving up their hold on her face, his hands ran down her delectable curves and scooped her up, placing her legs around his waist. He was beyond caring that to accommodate this position her skirt was pushed high onto her hips. He'd forgotten that Cindy might still be watching. All that mattered was reaching the nirvana this woman promised. He couldn't get close enough.

"Dude, take it home!" yelled Wilko from a distance, which was enough to make Robert come to his senses. Still holding Sophie wrapped around him, he opened the passenger door and deposited her on the seat. The sight of her parted, thoroughly kissed lips and panties showing beneath her rucked up skirt almost caused him to come undone.

"You're killing me woman."

CHAPTER 12

The sultry evening air rushed in through the open windows as Robert sped home. Sophie was resting her head back against the seat, feeling drugged with endorphins. What was it about this man that made her feel like this?

In another time and place she may have been mortified about the slick wetness between her legs, but right now she could only revel in it. Robert made her feel sexy. She totally lost any inhibitions around him, hence her encouraging their wild make out session in front of Cindy.

She smiled wryly as she admitted to herself that although she'd wanted Cindy to see her and Robert together, the heat of their kiss had quickly wiped the other woman's presence from her mind. The whole damn party could have been watching and Sophie couldn't have cared less. She ached to finally consummate this passion with Robert – it was driving her crazy.

He reached over and placed a large hand on her upper thigh, his thumb caressing her bare skin in tingly circles. Glancing away from the road he shot her a smoldering look, promising pleasure to come. Sophie couldn't tear her eyes away from him; his strong chiseled jaw in profile, his muscled forearm, elbow resting on the window frame and hand on the steering wheel – the night air running through his tousled hair.

No wonder he had women like Cindy falling over themselves to get to him. Sophie hated the thought of him having been with the voluptuous blonde, no matter how unreasonable. He deserved someone so much better than the two-faced bitch, how could he not see how conniving she was?

Cindy wasn't just working the whole blonde bombshell look, she was owning it; every pout of her lips and toss of her hair was a calculated move to raise the blood pressure of every male in a five-kilometer vicinity. More than one man there tonight had been covertly eyeing her curves.

It had physically pained her to see Cindy touching him, and not just because she was dying to get into his pants. She hated to think this kind, decent, beautiful man could end up with a woman who wouldn't appreciate all those qualities.

Sophie didn't want to mention Cindy to Robert again; she wanted his thoughts solely on what was to come when they got home. But she was curious about how long he had known her. Surely over the years he had to have pegged her for the woman she truly was under that sugar sweet smile?

How could he not?

What did that say about him that he was so set on being with a 'proper' country girl that he would, literally, settle?

And what did that mean he thought this was, with Sophie? Because she was clearly not the country girl ideal he was looking for.

Even though they had finite time together, Sophie wanted it to be more than just about the sex. She genuinely enjoyed his company and hoped he felt the same way… but maybe for him it was just about getting her into bed?

Argh, must stop thinking like this. I'm losing my glow.

As though he was tuned to her mood, Robert slid his hand higher until it sat beneath the hem of her skirt and gave a gentle squeeze. "Almost home."

As soon as he'd parked the ute he was out and around the vehicle to open Sophie's door. Although it was completely unnecessary he lifted her out and then let her body slide down his, his hands holding her against his hard, honed body.

She gasped involuntarily and tilted her head back to look at him, her hands automatically reaching up to wind around his neck. The throb between her legs kicked up and she absently wondered if she could get addicted to this kind of delicious tension.

They'd been hyper aware of each other for what seemed an eternity, and knowing the slow burn was about to combust was almost more than Sophie could bear.

"Take me inside. Now. Please," she all but whimpered.

He lowered his head fractionally, his words breathing into her mouth, "Oh baby, I'm going to take you all right. All night."

Pressed this close together, Sophie could feel his heart beating against her breast, desire radiating off him like heat. "Yes please."

With a growl he scooped her into his arms, striding towards the house. Cocooned against his chest, Sophie had never felt so delicate and feminine in her life. He vaulted up the veranda steps easily, lowering her to her feet at the door so he could open it.

Kicking off his boots he pulled her through and captured her mouth with his, strong arms encircling her. "Can't get close enough to you," he murmured in a gravelly voice. Impatiently, he picked her up again and didn't stop until he'd placed her standing at the foot of his bed. "It feels like I've been wanting you forever."

She didn't bother to respond, just tugged his head down again for more hungry kisses. He eased her backwards until her knees hit the bed and in one fluid motion she was on the mattress, him looming over her, his hands planted either side of her head.

They stilled, suspended untouching for a long moment – his arms holding him upright over her. The sweet agony threatened to send Sophie over the edge. She arched her back, thrusting her breasts towards Robert.

He needed no further invitation. He slung a leg over hers – trapping them – and reached up to loosely snare her wrists together in one large hand. Sophie whimpered in frustration. Knowing she craved contact, friction, release, Robert gave a wicked smile, "Slow it down kitten, we've got all night."

"I can't handle slow. Please Robert, I want to feel your weight on top of me."

He chuckled, but there was a dark edge of desire to the sound. "Soon baby, soon."

His free hand slipped beneath her t-shirt to knead her breast through the lacy cups of her bra, while his leg shifted to settle between hers. She rubbed herself shamelessly against him.

His rough palm smoothed down the sensitive skin of her stomach and undid the button of her skirt, dexterous fingers easing the zip down.

"I need to see every inch of you." Pulling her into a sitting position he pushed her t-shirt up and over her head, getting momentarily distracted by her pert breasts. Quickly he unclasped her bra and sighed in contentment as she was bared to him. Tugging off her boots he pulled her onto his lap to straddle him, pushing her skirt up around her waist. Hands splayed across her back, he arched her into him as he pulled a pebbled nipple into his mouth, sucking hard.

Sophie was lightheaded and grasping his hair as she flung her head back. His tongue was nipping, sucking, laving and she was falling apart in his arms. A calloused thumb swiped across her other nipple and her legs squeezed tighter around him. Without missing a beat he turned his attention to that breast and, cupping it, alternated between lapping with his tongue and tweaking the nipple between his thumb and finger.

Sophie could feel the pressure building and wanted, *needed*, him inside her. Clasping her hands behind his neck she fell backwards, pulling him with her so his weight crushed her down into the mattress. His leanly muscled bulk felt so good on her, she reveled in the weight but he propped up on an arm and smiled down at her.

"I haven't seen every inch yet. Not even close."

In defiance of her urgent panting, he leisurely moved his lips over hers, tasting and soothing and delving deep. Mindless, Sophie lost herself in his mouth, tongues tangling and sliding, her hands restlessly moving over his back and then up under his shirt, sliding over taut stomach muscles that quivered at her touch.

Her hands drifted higher and she grazed his nipples, smiling into his mouth when he moaned. Encouraged, she pinched them gently between her fingers and he stopped kissing her to moan again.

"Your shirt, it needs to be off," she whispered. She ached to see him shirtless; she wanted to be skin to skin with him. Yanking it up his body he shrugged the shirt over his head and threw it on the floor, grinning as she unconsciously licked her lips.

He was magnificent. Sophie had never been with a man

who exuded the raw male sexuality that Robert did. She wanted to bite him. His chest was broad and defined with muscles born of hard, manual work. The light dusting of hair was a sandy brown that trailed enticingly down his rock hard stomach.

He pressed her back onto the bed and she watched, fascinated, as he moved down her body, inhaling, kissing, biting, sucking, until he slid her skirt from her hips down, down, down her legs. He sat back on his haunches, admiring every curve and dip of her body, his eyes bright with lust.

"You are an absolute goddess." He drew in a ragged breath. "I wanted to drag this out, make it last, but I don't know that I can." He pulled her upright, settling her onto his lap again and she locked her ankles around him. She rocked then, sure and steady against the bulge in his jeans.

"We have all night for slow. Right now, I need you to take me," Sophie begged.

———

Robert was dangerously close to embarrassing himself. Sophie's arousal was luring him over the edge – he wanted nothing more than to bury himself inside her slick heat.

He had to keep his head. He wanted to make love to her – *with* her – he wanted their first time together to mean something.

But with her gorgeous breasts bouncing against his chest as she rubbed herself wantonly against his cock, Robert wasn't sure how much longer he could keep himself in check.

With a hand on her hip to slow her rocking grind, he

tangled a hand in the hair that was cascading down her back and licked first one nipple and then the other. Sophie had the most amazing body and the soft sweet sighs that fell from her lips had the blood pounding loudly in his ears.

He'd known she was beautiful, but to see her smooth legs wrapped around his waist, the flush in her cheeks and her kiss-swollen mouth… and those nipples… God, he could spend the rest of his life with those in his mouth and be a happy man.

"Rob, I need… I need more." She held eye contact while one of her small hands cupped his jaw and the other glided down between their bodies to rub herself through the satin of her panties.

"Soph, you're killing me. Show a little mercy," he groaned.

Flipping her off his lap he stood and hastily shucked his jeans and boxers. Still standing, he marveled at her luscious nakedness, propped up on her elbows with her hair falling over her breasts.

"You were definitely worth the wait," she grinned up at him, scooting forward until she was sitting in front of him. "And now it's my turn to taste you."

Hardly daring to breathe, Robert watched her take the thick length of him into her mouth, before sliding it back out, licking her way down and – maintaining eye contact – sliding her tongue back up.

Oh god, it felt amazing. Her wet mouth on his hot skin had his cock straining and his balls tightening. He put his hands lightly on the back of her head as she closed her eyes, taking him into her mouth, creating suction with her cheeks, drawing him further into her throat before sliding her mouth on and off him.

He was going to lose control.

"Babe, stop… now. I can't take any more."

He gripped her elbows and pulled away, falling back onto the bed while making sure not to crush her with his weight as he came down on top of her. The slide of their skin was incredible. She was so smooth and creamy and toned – she almost glowed beneath a light sheen of sweat...

"Are you ready for this?"

"I have never been more ready in my entire life. Please Robert, I need you in me."

He captured her mouth in another kiss, tasting rum and his own male scent, his fingers finding her moist center and dipping inside. Her hips bucked and she shuddered, clutching onto his forearm. Sliding his fingers out he quickly sheathed his erection with a condom and then slowly, slowly guided his length in until he filled her completely, stretching her tight.

They stilled, chest to chest, gazing into each other's eyes. Robert had never felt so connected to someone – as though they were truly one.

Slowly, slowly he withdrew until just his tip grazed her entrance, before rocking powerfully back into her. She opened her mouth in a wordless moan, fingers gripping onto his shoulders as she matched his rhythm with her hips, adjusting to his size and welcoming it fiercely.

He urged one of her knees up to allow for deeper penetration and she cried out his name, thrashing her head – she was going to leave bruises on his shoulders.

He couldn't hold back, the rocking became pounding and she matched him stroke for stroke. He wasn't going to last much longer and, needing her to come before he did, his hand slid between the slickness of their bodies to find that sensitive nub. One touch and she was shuddering around him, crying out her release. He thrust again and groaned deep and low as he spilled himself inside her.

Shuddering, he released the leg he'd been holding up and lowered to rest his body flush against hers, careful to keep his weight on his bent elbows against the mattress. That had been the single most shattering orgasm he had ever had. His head was actually spinning.

He rolled onto his side, bringing her with him so they remained entwined. Pressing slow, sated kisses over the top of Sophie's head he reveled in the closeness as she burrowed against his chest. He had never before felt this kind of intimacy with a woman. He pulled her closer.

He was surprised when she rolled apart and sat up, her hands going between her legs. "I'm, ah wet. Like really wet." Her voice was small and uncertain. "Shit Robert, I think the condom has broken," she cried as realisation dawned.

He snapped upright instantly.

Holy shit.

And yep, she was right. The latex was definitely split.

"Fuck. Hang on –" He jumped up to stride into the ensuite bathroom, disposing of the condom and taking a quick gulp of water from the tap.

This had never happened before – he was always careful when it came to protection. Hell, as well as the full box of condoms in the top drawer of his bedside table, he'd even stuffed a 'just in case' one into the pocket of his jeans before they'd gone out tonight.

Returning to the bed he lay down and pulled Sophie into his arms, resuming the gentle stroking of his hands down her arms, focusing on keeping it together.

"Are you on any kind of birth control?"

"No."

Okay, it's not the end of the world.

"We can always get the morning after pill tomorrow, right?"

Her big green eyes blinked up at him, wide with worry "I think we should be fine, it's not the right time in my cycle… It's just a shock. I've never had a condom break before."

"Me neither," he admitted. It was one hell of way to annihilate the post-coital glow.

She was tense in his arms, the languid bliss of moments ago gone. He wanted to reassure her, he wanted to re-capture that complete contentment he'd found within her.

He wanted to go back in time 20 minutes and choose a different damn condom.

"This is so not cool," she lifted her head and dropped it back onto his curled bicep in frustration. "I've always been so careful."

"It's okay, we'll sort it out," he said, pressing his forehead to hers. "For now, let's just enjoy this – the here and now."

CHAPTER 13

Although she'd set an alarm to wake her the next morning, Sophie was already wide eyed when it started beeping and was able to switch it off before it woke the still-slumbering man beside her. Lowering her head to rest again Robert's bicep, she resumed tracing patterns on his broad chest.

Last night had been incredible. They'd dozed off and awoken some time later, still clinging to each other, which resulted in an insane makeout session.

She had never kissed someone for such an extended period of time. Although kissing wasn't really the word for it; they'd inhaled each other. Her lips felt tender and swollen, and his stubble had left grazes on her sensitive skin. Her heart felt full in her chest – she'd never been so in-tune with someone before.

The slow loving he'd promised made her see stars – literally – at one point she'd felt like she may black out. It had almost been too much, she hadn't known whether the pleasure was actually pain. She'd needed to get away and she'd needed to get closer. And Robert had just kept on.

And on.

Release had been such a sweet surrender.

Between that and the excitement of her photography job with Lani, Sophie was way past any residual sleepiness, and even with the promise of pleasure that lay at her side, she was ready to get up.

The room was still dark as she slipped out of the bed, careful not to disturb Robert. She'd never really considered the practicalities of having children before, but when Lani had said that Archie woke at 5am, she'd had to hide a grimace. It was seriously early, even the sun wasn't up yet. She needed caffeine.

She bypassed the fancy coffee machine and went straight for instant – definitely not her preference but she had no idea how to work the slick silver appliance. She'd been tempted to leave a lipstick message scrawled on the bathroom mirror for Robert to find, but was suddenly shy about leaving such an obvious statement. And at this hour of the morning she couldn't think of anything witty to write.

She settled for a quick note on the kitchen bench:
Should only be at Lani's for a couple of hours. Miss you already.

The pen was poised to scratch out the 'miss you already' because really, it sounded a bit sappy. And definitely not something a fling would write.

But last night hadn't felt like a fling. Last night they'd melded together – there hadn't been anything flimsy or transient about it.

In the end, Sophie decided it would look bad to have scribbled something out, like she hadn't meant it when, in fact, she did. Missing his presence settled like an ache in her chest.

She reached into the back of the pantry and pulled out the almost-empty jar of Nutella she'd discovered a couple of mornings ago. It had been a little more full then. Two heaped spoonfuls of hazelnut chocolatey goodness was an excellent breakfast substitute. It intrigued her that Robert had a sweet tooth, she liked imagining him sucking the Nutella from a spoon…

She pulled herself together, she had a job to do.

Clutching the mud map Lani had drawn on the back of a paper napkin with directions to her farm, Sophie hopped up into the cab of Robert's ute and willed herself not to have forgotten how to drive a manual car. Turns out it was just like riding a bicycle, and she was cruising steadily down the back dirt roads in no time.

Lani and Henry lived on a property bordering one of Robert's southern paddocks, and their homestead was in much the same style as Robert's although its sprawling and manicured garden looked straight out of the pages of *House & Garden* magazine.

A walkway of purple wisteria vines led Sophie up onto their front verandah, where the door burst open and an energetic three-year old flung himself through, pulling up with a skid in front of Sophie's surprised face.

"Hi Sophie! I'm Archie. Mum's trying to brush my hair, but I hate it. Tell her I don't need it brushed," he demanded.

Lani followed at a more sedate pace, comb in hand. "Morning Soph, welcome to the mad house. Come on in and I'll just finish getting this monkey presentable."

Sophie grinned. Archie's white blonde hair looked as unruly as his behavior, and just as cute. He clutched ahold of her hand as their went into the house and whispered loudly, "It's okay, you can tell her I don't need it brushed. She'll listen to you."

Just then Henry bellowed from the kitchen, and both Sophie and Archie jumped. Knowing exactly what was causing the commotion, Archie decided it was safer to face his mother and fled to the bathroom.

"The bloody kid just spent all my money on four new headers!" Henry shook his own blonde head, so similar to his son's.

"Um, Archie? Bought a header?" Sophie was beyond confused.

"No, he bought *four* headers. He's got a thing for machinery, my son."

"I'm not sure I'm following you here. Archie seems a little young to be managing the farm's finances…"

A grin split Henry's face and Sophie all of a sudden saw exactly why Lani had fallen for this man – if she hadn't just left Robert's bed with the scent of their lovemaking still clinging, she'd almost be persuaded to compare.

"We've been playing a game, it's an app called Farming Simulator where you can manage a farm – plant and harvest crops, raise and sell stock. I had a healthy profit going and now Archie has gone and spent all the money on four New Holland combine harvesters."

"Like father like son," smiled Lani, leading a more subdued Archie, whose combed hair promptly fell back in his face. "Always wanting bright and shiny things."

Her eyes twinkled at her husband, and Sophie felt momentarily uncomfortable – these two made ordinary moments intimate with their obvious love. Her mind flashed to Robert, probably still blissfully asleep.

Yep, she missed him all right.

As suspected, Archie's antics kept the three of them entertained as Sophie moved them about in different locations throughout the verdant garden.

The early morning sun cast a gentle light as Sophie's lens clicked incessantly, capturing the boy's dancing eyes and flashing dimple, the soft looks shared between his parents and the glow emitted by the heavily pregnant Lani as she smoothed hands over her stomach.

The little family's sense of belonging, of togetherness, was tangible, and Sophie had to take a moment to swallow a lump in her throat. She hadn't known that she'd wanted this so badly.

She rubbed absently over her empty left ring finger, wondering if she could mourn something she'd never really had. She may have been engaged to be married, but even if the wedding had gone ahead, her marriage to Damien would never have had the depth she'd witnessed between Henry and Lani. And Damien had certainly never mentioned children.

Sophie was astounded she'd been prepared to spend the rest of her life with someone without having been sure she'd have children with them. Because all of a sudden the wanting of a baby – even one that woke at 5am – swamped her. Of course she wanted a baby. *Her* baby.

How had she never discussed this with Damien? Had she been so absorbed in the shallowness of their lifestyle that she would have risked never knowing this fact?

Had she really thought that being the darling of Sydney's high society was more fulfilling than raising a child?

It had already been six months since she'd called off her engagement, could she afford the luxury of waiting around having a fling with Robert, when she could be finding someone to share the rest of her life with? Didn't they say that once women reached a certain age, her fertility dropped rapidly?

The sudden earnestness of this primal urge had her head spinning. She felt that if she didn't grasp this now, it would pass her by. Would she ever know the feeling of carrying her own child? Breathe in the sweet newborn smell of her own flesh and blood?

In front of her, Archie continued to roll on the dew-wet lawn with his pet dog, and Henry held Lani's hand loosely as they chatted. They were oblivious to how their small family world had just collided with Sophie's and completely thrown her.

The quiet tranquility was broken with the harsh revving of a dirt bike roaring down the driveway.

"What the hell?" Henry moved fast to stand in front of his family, brows drawn down until he recognised Robert.

Sophie stood rooted to the ground. It was such an unexpected and overly loud sound, and she was already feeling dazed by her personal epiphany.

Robert practically leapt from the bike, its exhaust fumes lingering. "Are you okay?" he growled, stalking towards her and grabbing her to his chest. He buried his face in her neck and breathed deeply, his heart racing madly.

"I'm right here, I left you a note," she pulled slightly away to look him in the face. "Hey, I'm right here. You knew I was doing this job today."

Her confusion deepened. What was going on here?

"I checked the house phone's voice mail and there was a message from the local police station. Apparently the Sydney cops have been in contact, asking them to keep a look out for any strange vehicles in town. They were just touching base with us, but didn't say whether it was Damien they were looking out for, or –"

Lani and Henry and had turned discreetly away, and

Archie was enthralled with the dirt bike – it was just the two of them searching each other's face.

"Sorry, I guess I look a bit stupid barreling in here like this. I just had to find you." His eyes held hers, his hands still encircling her upper arms.

"Well I'm pretty sure we were just finishing here, weren't we Soph?" interrupted Lani with an understanding smile.

"Um yeah, we were. I think I've got some great shots. I'll email the proofs to you while you're away."

Sophie couldn't quite meet Lani's eyes. She had finished, and she was genuinely pleased with what she'd taken. But she was feeling shaken by her own revelation and the abrupt arrival of Robert.

Who was the stranger the police were expecting?

"I'm going to pop some lemonade scones in the oven, did you want to stay for a cuppa? Actually," Lani looked between Sophie and Robert, "I'm pretty sure you both probably need to get going." She hid a smile but her eyes crinkled kindly at the corners; she was completely unaware of the potential threat, no doubt believing it was lust that was driving Robert.

"Yeah, I think we do. Sorry for the interruption Lani. Henry, mind if I leave my bike in your shed and drive Soph home in the ute?"

"Sure man, no problem." He too, was hiding a grin. "I'll put it away for you. You and Sophie get on out of here."

———

If Robert hadn't been so relieved to find Sophie safe with Lani and Henry, he may have been embarrassed at his rash behavior in charging over there.

But when the officer who'd left the message hadn't been available to take Robert's responding call, he'd felt compelled to find her. Until they knew exactly what was going on, he wasn't taking any chances.

He'd woken up this morning after hands down the best sex he'd ever had in his life, to find the bed beside him empty and cold.

He'd been looking forward to feeling her snuggled against his side, to teasing her about her bed hair and having a leisurely shower together. He hadn't stopped to think that these were all things you didn't do with a fling, he'd just missed her, and then completely freaked out when he'd listened to that voice message. His blood had literally run cold.

He shook his head to clear his thoughts. She was here beside him, safe. He glanced across at her and then back at the road. The depth of his feelings for her was unsettling. It was too soon, too much, too strong.

This was temporary. He could handle that. He wasn't getting attached, not even close. He just wanted to maximize the time they had together, that was all.

Speaking of which, he pulled over to the side of the deserted dirt road into the shade of an Iron Bark tree and pulled on the handbrake.

"I'm pretty pissed you left without a goodbye kiss," he growled, unbuckling his seatbelt and leaning over to un-do hers as well. "You've got some serious making up to do kitten."

She raised her eyebrows and smirked at him; "Any time, any place, cowboy." She lost the smirk rapidly when he grabbed her around the waist and hauled her onto his lap.

Before she could quite comprehended what was happening, he'd moved his seat back and was driving his tongue into her mouth, his hands in her hair keeping her head still.

She moaned into his mouth and opened for him fully, her own hands wound into his hair. There was no finesse to this, it was purely raw passion – he wanted to brand her with his mouth.

"I didn't like waking up alone baby. I wanted you hot and wet and ready. You hot and wet and ready now?"

His lips moved to the sensitive spot behind her ear, and then he closed his teeth around the ear lobe. She gasped. Nuzzling her neck he smoothed his hands down and pushed the straps of her dress off her shoulders, leaving only a satin strapless bra between him and the divine breasts beneath.

He was beyond grateful for her collection of lingerie but, at times like this, it was entirely unnecessary. Making quick work of the clasp he had her bare and in his hands, caressing and kneading – fingers brushing ever so lightly over her hardened nipples as she arched her back, pushing herself into him.

Shifting slightly he pulled his own shirt over his head and tossed it aside, needing to feel her skin against his. His hand cupped her satin–covered sex and she ground against it.

"Robert, please. I need more." Her cheeks were flushed the same rosy colour as her nipples and as she pushed both his hands down to her heat she raised her own hands to cup her breasts.

The woman was his every fantasy come to life. He smiled, knowing it looked slightly feral with its intensity. "Okay baby. Okay."

Chest to chest, she straddled him, riding his hand as his

fingers delved deep inside her, stroking her until she was teetering on the edge of oblivion. Their foreheads pressed together, hot breath panting into each other's mouth. She closed her eyes and clenched her internal muscles around his fingers, so close. And then his thumb circled the sensitive nub of her clit and she threw her head back in an agony of ecstasy.

"That's right babe, come for me on my hand."

She shuddered and collapsed against his chest, breathing heavily, hands still clutching his shoulders. Yep, there'd definitely be bruises.

He grinned. "You know if you hadn't left me this morning, this wouldn't be your first orgasm of the day."

"Mmmmm. Better late than never," she replied lazily, not bothering to open her eyes.

"I found your phone in the kitchen when I tried to call you before coming over to the Mayberry's, and there was a message from Sara on the screen…"

He knew she'd sit up when he said that.

"And…?"

"She asked how the "yummy cowboy" was."

"Oh he's pretty damn delicious."

Having assured Sophie that he could wait to achieve his own release until they reached a bed – as opposed to the cramped confines of the ute – Robert had tested the vehicle's speed capacity on his way home.

Only to be bailed up on the homestead driveway by Jono on a four-wheel bike, needing help pulling heifers from a dam.

As Jono rode off to get more rope from the shed, Robert

clenched his fists around the steering wheel and dropped his head to bang against it, groaning.

"You have to be kidding. The world is conspiring against me."

"Nope, just some cows. Someone once told me that anticipation is even better than recollection. Get out there and save some cows, and I'll be waiting for you when you get back."

"It's okay for you to be so cheery, you're not the one with a zipper imprint on your cock. You're going to be the death of me woman."

She snorted with laughter, and then slapped a hand over her mouth in mortification. "I can't believe I just snorted."

"I can't believe I'm leaving you here to have a shower by yourself, and I'm heading out to pull cows out of mud."

He was only half joking. And that worried him. The farm had always come first for him. Nothing had ever been more important than ensuring everything ran as well as it could on his patch of the world.

He'd even missed a cousin's wedding several years ago because sowing had been slowed down with mechanical problems. He always prided himself on having his priorities in order.

Farm first. Life second. Although to be honest, the farm pretty much *was* his life.

He brooded over this as he dropped Sophie at the homestead and headed out to one of the southern paddocks. Living on the farm was lonely – he wanted someone to share it with. But had that single-minded focus eclipsed finding the *right* person? He'd thought because he and Cindy had a friendship and a shared background that they could make it work together. And hell, maybe they could.

But after experiencing the chemistry that flared between he and Sophie? He didn't think he could settle for a woman who didn't inspire that in him. A woman who *he* didn't inspire passion in. Half the turn-on with Sophie was knowing he was driving her crazy with desire.

But he knew better than to think a city girl like Sophie would stay out here on the farm permanently. They were two different. Even sizzling chemistry wouldn't change that.

Although with Damien's scheming, would there even be a farm to stay on?

It still stung to remember the phone call from the local ag store, who regretfully explained his cheque for the latest load of fertilizer had bounced. Robert was never late with a payment and always on top of his finances, so he'd been confused rather than humiliated.

At first.

That was before he called the bank, who'd informed him that the other signatory on the farm's bank account – his brother – had just withdrawn $300,000. Money that was already allocated to pay the inputs for that season's crops, and another AI program for his cattle.

The farm and its bank accounts had been in both Robert and Damien's names ever since their parent's estate had been settled. And because Damien had never touched the farm money, Robert hadn't seen the need to change anything – assuming her even could. Besides, as distant as their relationship may have become, Damien was still his brother. He'd trusted him.

So the sly withdrawal from the bank account – and the resulting impact on Robert's breeding program – grated.

Hard.

Extending the overdraft based on the farm's equity wasn't something that Robert had wanted to do, but with invoices waiting to be paid he hadn't had a choice. And now Damien was pushing for part of the farm to be sold. He hadn't even contacted Robert to ask if he could buy him out. Probably because he knew Robert couldn't take on that much debt. It just wasn't feasible with the earning capacity of the land.

Which left Robert hanging, unsure about the future of everything. Come to think of it, now was sure as hell not the time to be thinking about sharing this lifestyle with any woman.

Even one as tempting as Sophie.

CHAPTER 14

Sophie's leg was braced over Robert's shoulder and he was thrusting deep – a sheen of sweat slicking their bodies as they slammed against each other, fast, faster. With her pelvis tilted forward like this Robert's thick length penetrated deep with each slide of his hips, and if it didn't feel so damn good it would hurt.

Actually, it felt so good that it *did* hurt.

Sophie was flushed from their exertion and breathless from the intimacy of their eyes locked on each other. She had never felt so connected to someone, and not just where their bodies were joined.

The police had reassured them it was Damien they were looking out for, but had advised she continue to stay at the farm and away from Sydney, and last week they'd spent practically every single minute together – either tangled in bed or out on the farm. She couldn't get enough of Robert, even when they were doing something as mundane as throwing hay bales off the back of the ute to feed cattle.

In fact, watching the strength in his broad shoulders and heavily muscled arms as he toiled did quivery things to her inside.

In just two short weeks the man had embedded himself on her indelibly. Even before they had kissed, there had been a current between them. An awareness. And now their physical bond had forged that consciousness into something she was afraid to define.

The idea of this being a fling, of leaving this man one day in the future, made her feel nauseous. Her mind blanked when she tried to think of what she'd do with her life when she left the farm behind and headed back to the city. Robert, and his life here on the farm, consumed all her headspace – she couldn't see beyond it.

Didn't know if she wanted to.

All thought was obliterated when Robert released her leg and she locked her ankles around his waist – holding him close. His chest flush with hers, bracing his weight on his forearms, he cupped her face with his hands and lowered his lips to take hers feverishly. She matched his rocking rhythm thrust for thrust, fingers digging into his back.

Her orgasm built. She couldn't hold out against the force of their passion for much longer. Just one swipe of his thumb over her clit and she bucked against him, gasping and whimpering as pleasure pulsed through her whole body. She thrummed with the carnality of her orgasm and saw stars. A whole damn galaxy of them. This passion between them was beyond comprehension.

His release followed immediately, a groan falling from his mouth as he dropped his head into the crook of her neck – his sated body crushing her into the mattress.

She loved the weight of him stretched out on top of her. She wanted to crawl into his skin.

"You rock my world," he whispered, licking the damp skin of her neck and rolling off her, bringing her with him to nestle against his side.

With his hands smoothing up and down her back she felt a profound contentment. She could stay here like this, feeling his calloused hands on her skin and breathing in the scent of their lovemaking, forever.

"I don't want to move. I think I'll just stay here like this for the next week, 'kay?" she murmured.

"No can do kitten. I've promised I'll be at the pub tonight for the head wetting of Stephen's baby, and you said you'd go to Michelle's Tupperware party."

"Are you even allowed to take a baby to the pub?"

"The baby is still in hospital with its mother. A head wetting is a way to celebrate the birth with alcohol – basically an excuse for Stephen to get drunk. Which he probably needs after witnessing his wife in labour."

"I'm pretty sure his wife needs the alcohol more than he does after having given birth."

Her mind flashed to the fact that they'd been too caught up in each other the day after the condom broke to think about whether they should take the precaution of the morning after pill. Her cycle was regular and she knew her body well – the timing meant they were safe. But that didn't stop a little niggle of worry…

Robert laughed at her and pulled back a little so he could look into her face. "You're probably right, I'm very sure the labour was harder for her than it was for him," he sobered slightly, running his finger over the seam of her lips. "I think it would be incredibly hard seeing someone I love go through the pain of childbirth."

"Does that mean you don't want children?"

Sophie held her breath wondering if she even wanted to know the answer. When had she started to unconsciously dream of her future baby having Robert's dimples?

Shit, I am getting in way over my head with this man.

His gaze drifted over her shoulder and he studied the wall, before carefully saying, "Not right now."

Why did it feel like he'd just bruised her heart when he said that? Since when was her heart even involved in this?

He kissed her on the forehead and disentangled their legs, getting to his feet. She couldn't keep her eyes off his delicious ass as he ambled into the adjoining bathroom, tying off the condom and depositing it in the bin.

Sophie rolled onto her stomach and buried her face in the pillow, which smelt of his clean, masculine scent that, incredibly, started a throb between her legs. Again.

This man had made her insatiable.

She needed to get her head sorted asap, and file Robert back under the 'short term' category. She'd never been the clingy type, and she was determined to refocus and banish this interlude with Robert as just that, a moment in time.

An amazing moment – which may just ruin her for all men for all time – but a moment nonetheless.

Of course he wasn't going to be her baby daddy. There wasn't going to be a Happily Ever After with the man who was once-upon-a-time going to be her brother-in-law. The sooner she moved on from this, the better.

Although surely a few more nights in his bed couldn't hurt?

Sophie was sitting on Michelle's lounge as the Tupperware lady did her sales pitch. The other women in the room were hanging on her every word, and were going nuts over a new pressure cooker.

Sophie was trying to keep her bemusement to herself –

she'd actually never been to a Tupperware party before, but they seemed to be all the rage in this country town.

Now a lingerie party, *that* is something she'd been to.

"I can't believe this is your first Tupperware party!" exclaimed Michelle, happily filling out an order form for something called a Speedy Chef. "I'm not even sure what I'm going to cook with this – but I *need* it."

Sophie smiled into her champagne glass and continued to look around the room. It was a far remove from her social life in Sydney, but she felt surprisingly comfortable. What the room lacked in designer décor, it made up for with personal touches and a homey atmosphere; the women weren't wearing the latest fashions to trip off the runways, but they expressed a genuine happiness that left Sophie with a yearning for… something.

She felt a twinge at the familiarity that a shared upbringing in a small town had engendered. These women knew each other. And they enjoyed spending time with each other. It made her miss Sara fiercely, although not the endless string of invitations to Sydney's hottest events.

The twinge in her tummy turned to a wave of nausea, which swept through her unexpectedly and left her clammy and shaky. She hated feeling in limbo with her life, and wasn't surprised that it was manifesting itself physically. With her brain in so much turmoil, who could blame her body for following suit?

She was jolted back to the present by Andrea, whose effervescent personality reminded Sophie of Sara. She was long overdue for a catch up with her bestie.

"So I know Michelle told us we weren't allowed to ask you about Robert, but girl we are *dying* to know what's going on between you two."

Michelle threw a cushion at Andrea, and the Tupperware lady paused in her demonstration of the professional knife set. Just as well, because all attention was now firmly fixed on Sophie's face, which she just knew was blushing.

"You do *not* have to answer that Sophie, Andrea is just being nosy," said Michelle, but her eyes betrayed her own eagerness.

"Are you together?" pushed Andrea.

"Yes, we're seeing each other," Sophie hedged. "For now. It's not permanent; I'll be heading back to Sydney soon. It just kind of happened."

"I'd let him happen to me too," sympathized Andrea. "What?!" she exclaimed when another cushion was aimed her way. "Don't tell me his charming smile hasn't had anyone else's knickers in a knot."

"Wilko told me that he hadn't ever seen Robert get worked up over a girl before," confided Michelle. "Apparently he was ready to punch Wilko just for talking to you."

"He knew Wilko wasn't being serious," assured Sophie. "He can get kind of worked up, but we're just, you know, having fun…"

"He's so intense it's HOT," sighed Andrea. "I want a gorgeous man going all caveman over me."

"Oh god, speaking of cavemen, until Wilko's barbeque I hadn't seen Henry Mayberry in ages. And that man just gets better with age. Doesn't it just *kill you* how insanely in love with Lani he is?"

"I actually just took some family photographs for them," said Sophie, "And it's impossible not to see how in love they are."

I am not *feeling wistful.*

"Oh god, did she make you her lemonade scones? They're to die for, seriously. She's given me the recipe and even when I follow it word for word I still can't make mine the way hers taste," said Michelle enviously.

"Lani's scones are not what I'm fantasizing about." Andrea sighed dramatically again, "But she definitely gives a girl hope for their own knight in shining armour."

———

Robert chugged back a schooner of beer, as the new father shouted another round and proposed yet another toast to his newborn son.

"May you all have the good fortune of producing a son and heir!" His beer sloshed as unsteady hands raised the glass into the air.

Robert noted Stephen's slightly panicked eyes hiding behind his good cheer, and he decided he'd be getting drunk too, if he'd just become responsible for a newborn. Even the thought made his palms slippery with sweat. He'd never actually held a new baby before, and the thought of doing so made him as nervous as a whore in church.

He thought back to earlier, when Sophie had asked him about wanting kids. He was definitely ready to settle down, but babies were taking that to a whole other level that he just wasn't sure he was ready for.

He slapped Stephen heartily on the back, "Better you than me mate."

"It was brutal mate, bloody brutal. I think this little fella will be an only child," confided Stephen, placing the back of his hand over his mouth to cover a belch. "And he cries. All the time. Bloody healthy set of lungs on him."

Robert laughed, his eyebrows raised in pity. "Like I said, better you than me."

He headed over to the pool table, where Wilko and a couple of the boys had a game going. Idly he wondered if Sophie knew how to play pool; he'd love to bend her over a pool table…

Christ, I can't even stop thinking about her at the pub!

It was definitely a concern, this obsession with her. And it was an obsession; he'd never felt so compelled by a female. His chest felt tight when he thought of her, he wanted to constantly have his hands on her delectable body. He'd hindered her so much while she tried to cook breakfast this morning that she'd kicked him out of his own kitchen.

Damn but the woman had some amazing curves.

"Don't look now mate, but Cindy just came in through the side door and she's making her way over here," said Wilko with a smirk. "And she's dressed to impress."

Robert slowly swiveled to face the oncoming woman, who was swinging her hips in a sultry sway. And yeah, her low-cut top did showcase her superb breasts. But he noted this with detachment, because her chest just didn't have the allure it used to.

Not when he had images of Sophie's perfectly puckered nipples and creamy, plump cleavage on constant rotation in his head.

He drained his beer so he had an excuse to avoid her approach, and headed back to the bar. Cindy had made it clear she didn't want more from a relationship with him, and he'd moved on. Happily. He should probably be thanking her, rather than avoiding her.

Propping himself against the bar he ordered Stephen a top-shelf rum, and decided he needed one himself.

"Your little friend isn't with you tonight," purred Cindy, pulling herself onto the barstool next to him. "Or has she already headed back to the big city and you're here to drown your sorrows?"

She gave Robert a playful shove, leaving her hand to linger on his bicep. "Because I can help you with that, you know."

"Her name is Sophie, and she's at Michelle's. I'm here for Stephen – he and Carly had a baby boy last night." Robert put his rum onto the bar and turned to face Cindy, which only encouraged her to run one of her crossed over legs up his own.

"Regardless, the offer still stands. We always had a good time, you and me."

"No, Cindy." He placed a firm hand on her leg and pushed it gently aside. "I don't want to be an asshole here, but what we had was in the past, and you're the one who put it there. I'm with Sophie now and, even if she heads back to Sydney, you and I have had our time."

"*If* she heads back?" Cindy raised an eyebrow.

"When."

Am I correcting Cindy, or myself?

The cover band in the corner started to belt out Cold Chisel's *Flame Trees* and Cindy nodded at him. "Okay then, but I think you at least owe me one last dance, for old times sake."

She'd lost her playful edge and Robert swore she almost looked sad. Jesus, he was a soft touch. "Sure, one last dance."

He led her onto the makeshift dance floor, which was filling up with slowly swaying couples and pulled her into his arms. She moved closer and he was joltingly aware of how wrong she felt in his embrace. He'd grown accustomed to the size and fit of Sophie against him, her sweet vanilla scent and her big green eyes blinking up at him.

Cindy felt all kinds of wrong – she was too tall, too busty and her musky perfume too strong. He stopped moving and placed his hands on her shoulders, straightening his arms to create distance between their bodies. "I'm sorry Cindy, I can't do this," and he strode from the pub.

Sophie had her legs tucked under her on the passenger seat and was adorably sleepy as she fought to keep her eyes open on the drive home.

"It's okay kitten, just rest your head back. We'll be home in no time."

"No, no. I want to keep you company. I can help you look for kangaroos on the road. You haven't had too much to drink, have you?"

"I'm not over the legal limit, don't worry. And if I was, there are no taxis out here in the bush to drive us home, so we'd have to stay the night in town."

"Really? I knew Minnippi was small, but I still thought there'd be a taxi. Wow, I'm really not in Kansas anymore, am I Toto?"

He reached out to brush a finger affectionately against her cheek. So goddamn smooth… he really should let her catch up on sleep tonight, the lack over the last few nights had caught up with her.

"Who was at the pub tonight?" Her voice was suddenly less sleepy, and she was watching him closely.

"Just a few of the guys, the usual crowd."

"No women?"

"Well, it was a normal night at the pub, so sure – there were women there. Why?"

"You smell of women's perfume."

Ah hell. He so did not want to mention Cindy's name. It was beyond over between them, and he didn't want to create conflict over a non-event.

He didn't want Sophie tense, he wanted to carry her into bed and spoon in behind her, stroking and caressing her into sweet dreams. Preferably of him.

"Baby, of course I talked to the women there. This is a small town, I grew up with half of them. You're not jealous are you?" he smiled winningly at her and flashed his dimple, which he knew she couldn't resist. "You should know I find your being covetous very sexy."

"I'm surprised you even know big words like covetous," she grumbled, hiding a smile. "You're having a shower before you get into bed – I don't want you making our sheets smell of some other woman's perfume."

He liked the way she called them 'our' sheets.

Hell yes.

CHAPTER 15

After calling the solicitor again, Robert had to wait several days for an appointment, days that Sophie spent trying to distract him. She could see how much the uncertainty of the situation was eating at him, and was so angry with Damien for trying to force the sale of part of the property.

She knew her ex-fiancé was selfish, but this was just beyond comprehension – especially as he didn't have the guts to face Robert in person, and he'd yet to return their phone calls.

They'd had further word from the police, who confirmed they weren't treating Damien as a missing person, and they weren't concerned for his safety after a tip off that the people he'd owed money to had been paid. No, they were now far more interested about where that money had come from.

And as the money hadn't come from the farm, Sophie had to assume he'd obtained it through financial trading. She'd never been interested enough to really understand the finer details of his career.

Over the last couple of weeks she had seen first hand how dedicated Robert was to the land. How it defined him as a man and how much he loved it. Hell, the tranquility and beauty of the place was even getting to *her* – she couldn't imagine how it must feel to have the possibility of losing it looming over him.

Since the police had declared there was no danger in

returning to Sydney, Sophie and Robert had skirted the issue of exactly how much longer she'd be staying at the farm. Because while it might be safe to go back, she didn't have a home or a job to return to… and they were enjoying each other so much…

Looking now at his head bent over *The Land* newspaper, morning sunlight spilling through the window highlighting his strong jawline she felt her heart swell in her chest. His dark hair was curling ever so slightly over the top of his ears, his large hands grasping a coffee mug. He was such a raw, virile, beautiful man – his physical presence still gave her butterflies in her stomach.

And the way he treated her? Like she was a queen. He stroked her gently, and teased her mercilessly. He looked at her affectionately and respected her opinions. Took her hard, and took her slow. He was the total goddamn package.

Just yesterday he had cornered her in the kitchen, playfully demanding to know why his jar of Nutella was practically empty. Sophie blushed remembering how she'd swiped the last of the chocolate hazelnut spread over his erection, and used her mouth to suck it clean. She'd loved how his stomach muscles had clenched and his hands had held the back of her head, encouraging her with groans of pleasure.

She was never going to look at Nutella the same again.

"What are you blushing about over there kitten?" He had looked up from his newspaper, eyeing her with a wicked glint as though he could read her mind.

Oh god I hope not.

Because Sophie was slowly coming to the realisation that this was way more than just a fling for her; her emotions for the man were out of control crazy. She couldn't help but think about forever with him.

"Get your delectable butt over here. You haven't eaten nearly enough breakfast, let me feed you," he demanded.

She settled herself in his lap, wiggling her bottom a little more than necessary because his arousal was making itself known. Linking her hands behind his neck she pulled him down so she could nibble on his bottom lip.

"I'm not really hungry for food…"

"One orgasm wasn't enough for you this morning huh?"

"Well if you insist on getting about the house without a shirt on, I can't be held responsible for my actions."

She *loved* his bare chest. It was broad and had just the right amount of hair, his muscles clearly defined and clearly begging for her touch. She was more than happy to oblige.

Slinging one leg over his lap to sit astride him, she leaned an elbow back against the kitchen table, her other hand running lazily up and down his chest, a finger idly twirling around his nipple. She knew this position pushed her breasts up and out, and judging by the fact Robert couldn't take his eyes off the straining nipples visible beneath her singlet, he liked it.

Very much.

"Well I think it's only fair that if I'm not wearing a top, you shouldn't either."

She grinned and raised her arms obediently. He slipped his fingers under the hem and in one fluid movement pulled it over her head and dropped it carelessly to the floor.

Both his hands cupped her exposed breasts. Pushing them together he ran the pads of his thumbs over her hardened nipples reverently. She watched him with hooded eyes, his touch pooling heat instantly between her legs.

"You are so damn beautiful."

"Rob take me now. I need to feel you inside me."

He stood and slid her down his rock hard body, turning her to face the table, placing her palms flat in front of her. Hands she couldn't see pulled her shorts and panties down and nudged her legs apart. Naked and trembling with anticipation, she waited for his next move.

"Stay there, and don't move. I'll be right back."

The throbbing in her core intensified – she was so hot for this man. The wait was wickedly delicious. He returned in seconds and Sophie watched over her shoulder as he quickly sheathed his impressive length with a condom.

Large hands gripped her hips and in a single plunge he was tight within her, filling her completely. A gasp tore from her throat and before she could draw breath he had pulled out and slammed back in again.

This is what she needed, what she craved. She wanted to him to take her hard and rough. His pounding, rocking force hit that elusive pleasure spot and already her orgasm was building.

Abruptly Robert changed his rhythm, slowing until he pulled out completely, teasing her entrance with the tip of his cock.

"I'm close babe, I just need to slow it down. Take it easy."

"No! I don't want easy, damn you," she growled, frustration making her voice cottony and stick in her throat. She was burning up with need.

"Want to beg me for it?" But his voice was just as thick, and at her answering, pleading mew he thrust back in to his hilt, taking her without mercy.

In moments she was shuddering around him, her insides

clenching his cock as a powerful orgasm ripped through her. The force of pleasure consumed her. Obliterated everything but the feel of Robert as he took her.

Dazed, she was riding breaking waves of her orgasm when he removed one hand from her hip and inserted it between her legs, his clever fingers homing in on her swollen clit.

One tweak and she was flying high again, her toes curling into the floor and her heels lifting, pushing her higher into Robert's oncoming thrusts.

One more stroke, two and he followed her, crying out his own release as he rocked them to completion.

Sophie walked the supermarket aisles in a slight daze, unable to concentrate on her grocery list while Robert's clean, masculine scent clung to her and each step reminded her of the pleasant ache between her legs.

She stopped in front of a shelf stocked with Nutella and put three jars into the shopping trolley. She also grabbed a pack of mint chewing gum; she'd felt car sick on the drive into town, and hoped the gum would starve off the nausea.

When she'd first visited the supermarket she'd been dumbfounded. She knew Minnippi wasn't big enough for a major supermarket, but she'd seen corner stores in Sydney bigger than this. Out here, fresh fruit and vegetables were delivered once a week, which meant if you timed your visit wrong you'd be left with a choice of wilted spring onions or browning broccoli. She was prepared this week, and was happily rewarded with fully stocked shelves.

Browsing the fruit section she reached for the strawberries, which she had a sudden craving to devour here and now.

Which was funny because she'd never really had a taste for them.

Thinking about taste, had Sara told her something once about men who ate fresh pineapple having sweet tasting semen? She put a pineapple into the cart.

"Oh look, it's the city slicker," cooed a soft voice from behind.

Sophie spun around and narrowed her eyes when she saw Cindy, sans trolley and empty handed. Intuitively Sophie just *knew* Cindy wasn't here to shop – she must have seen Sophie enter the supermarket alone and followed her inside.

There goes my happy glow. Bitch.

Sophie grit her teeth and said nothing, waiting to see what Cindy was up to. She didn't have to wait long.

"I'm surprised you're still here. I didn't think you'd be into sharing your man. I know I'm not. Into sharing, that is." Cindy was smug as she waited for Sophie's response, folding her arms under her breasts to push them up further.

Seriously, could she put her boobs away already?

Sophie refused to bite. She trusted Robert when he said there was nothing between he and Cindy anymore. And even though she was livid that Cindy's mouth had been anywhere near Robert's body, she wasn't going to give the woman the satisfaction of knowing how affected she was.

"So you don't mind that Robert and I were together again last weekend?" Cindy raised an eyebrow and smirked. "I hate to be the one to upset you, but I guess old habits die hard. Robert and I have a lot of history together, and he just can't stay away."

Sophie gripped tighter to her shopping trolley and swallowed. Robert had reeked of perfume after being at the pub and what do you know? It was the same scent that clouded Cindy now. She didn't believe, *couldn't* believe, that he'd been intimate with Cindy, but if he'd seen her at the pub, why hadn't he said so when she'd asked him which women had been there?

If he had nothing to hide, why hadn't he mentioned seeing her?

——

"Are you fucking kidding me?" Robert's voice exploded around the corner as he stalked towards them, hands clenched into fists and wearing an incredulous expression. "You *know* nothing happened between us at the pub."

Cindy flushed, clearly rattled, but he refused to back down. She was purposely jeopardizing his relationship with Sophie and it made him mad as hell; the fact that Sophie was white as a sheet and seemed to be using her shopping trolley to stay on her feet made his blood boil.

Swiftly he moved behind Sophie and tugged her back to rest against his chest, glaring in confusion at Cindy as he put his arms proprietarily around her.

He calmed slightly when Sophie relaxed into his body and he took a deep breath, trying to decide what the hell was going on here.

"Why would you say something like that to Sophie, when nothing happened?"

Cindy widened her eyes innocently but no way was he falling for that bullshit. He'd finished early at the hardware store and had been in the next aisle over looking for Sophie and he'd heard the tone in Cindy's voice, which was almost worse than the words.

"It wasn't *nothing* Robert! You held me and we danced together. You can't tell me you don't feel something for me!"

"God, I think I'm going to be sick," muttered Sophie, holding a hand over her mouth. "I don't need to hear this. Robert, can you take what's in the trolley to the cash register? I'm going to wait outside."

She shrugged out of his grasp and almost sprinted for the exit. Every instinct urged him to follow her, to reassure her and make sure she was okay. But he needed to sort this out with Cindy once and for all, it had gone on for long enough.

He stepped forward into Cindy's personal space and his voice was low and measured as he hissed into her surprised face. "There is nothing between us. *You* decided that, and *I'm* sticking to it. If you so much as glance in Sophie's direction again, you will seriously regret it. I don't know why you've changed your mind, and to be honest, I don't really care. But this ends now."

The young girl at the checkout took forever to scan the few items that Sophie had wanted, and Robert had to force himself to wait with some semblance of patience. In his current state he was likely to detonate with little provocation.

Sophie's pale face and trembling hands were embedded in his mind and he was burning up knowing she was upset. He just hoped it was because of Cindy's intimidation antics, and not the actual words she'd spoken. Surely Sophie couldn't think he'd done anything with Cindy?

Although I did dance with her. Stupid, stupid, stupid.

The minor confrontation that may have occurred in the car had he told Sophie about the dance was nothing compared to how it looked now, when he hadn't told her at all. God*damn*.

He slowed when he reached the vehicle, not sure how he would find Sophie. It *killed him* that she was unhappy.

"Babe, you okay?"

The passenger door was open and she was sitting there with her legs swinging out, some colour back in her face, her eyes sad.

"Why didn't you tell me you'd danced with her?"

"I should have, I am so sorry. It was stupid not to tell you. I just didn't want to upset you when it was just a dance, and I didn't even finish the song – I realised it felt wrong and I left the pub."

"Her shoving my face in the fact upset me a whole lot more than you telling me would have."

"I know, and I'm sorry." He stood between her legs and framed her face with his hands, tilting it up so he could brush his lips over her forehead, down her temple, across her lips.

"What can I do to make you feel better?"

"Pass me the chewing gum, I'm feeling queasy."

"Still car sick?"

"Probably more Cindy sick now," she grumbled, grinning weakly at him and shading her eyes from the glaring sun. "I need to get into some air-conditioning, it's hotter than Hades out here. What time is the appointment with the solicitor?"

"We've got 10 minutes." Putting the groceries into the back he got behind the steering wheel and cranked the air-conditioning. "Mind telling me why you bought a whole pineapple?"

Martin Lawrence had been Robert's family's solicitor for decades and he rose from behind his desk as they entered his office, warmly shaking Robert's hand.

"Robert my boy, it's been a while." He continued to pump Robert's hand and brought his other up to clasp over the top of their joined ones. "Although it's a sorry business that's brought you here."

Dropping his ample body back behind the desk he took off his glasses and rubbed at the lenses absently, his attention moving to Sophie.

"Hello there. And who might you be?"

"This is Sophie. Sophie Richards. She was Damien's fiancé."

"So you're here representing Damien's interests?"

"No!" she protested hotly, her gaze flying between the two men.

"No, she's here with me." Robert's statement was firm, his arm settling across the back of Sophie's chair.

Martin eyed the two of them with interest. "Well then. And Robert you're fine for Sophie to hear what we speak about today?"

Robert leaned back in his chair and stretched his legs out. He'd never shared his financial concerns with anyone outside of a professional capacity, and he'd expected to feel some kind of reservation doing so now.

But it felt absolutely right to have Sophie by his side. As much as he hated that her life was turned upside down and she'd been in danger, it was good to know they were in this together.

"Totally fine." He reached across and snagged Sophie's hand in his, holding it tight. There was one good thing that had come of this; if Damien hadn't fucked up so spectacularly he would never had had this chance with her.

"Okay then. This is how I see it. Damien has contacted a real estate agent to facilitate the sale of half of Acacia Ridge, and we have been instructed to have contracts drawn up for its sale. Because you own the property as joint tenants, that is that the property was left in a 50-50 share between you on the death of your parents, he is technically within his legal rights to do so. As you know, however, your parents included a clause in their will that stipulated if either one of you wanted to sell your share of the property, the other brother was to have the first option of buying the other one out. Apparently Damien is aware of this, but for reasons unknown has commissioned an agent to list the property on the open market for sale."

Although Martin's words were factual, Robert could sense the elderly man's distaste for Damien's actions. This was old news to Robert; he wanted to know what he could do to circumvent a sale.

"But surely he can't sell half the property to someone else if Rob doesn't agree?" Sophie interrupted.

"As half owner, he can. I suggest we set up a mediation to see if we can't work around the need to sell."

Robert growled in frustration, running his free hand through already mussed hair; "We can't do mediation if we can't get in contact with him. He's ceased all communication and we don't know where he is."

"If we could get him to agree to mediation, what are the options?" Sophie quietly asked, trying to steer the conversation ahead.

"The most likely would be for Robert to purchase

his brother's share of the land, but to pay Damien out in installments."

"I'm already paying him a more than generous lease payment in installments. He doesn't want that. What he wants is a large chunk of cash upfront," sighed Robert.

"Should I ask what he needs this money for?"

"He owes money to some bookies. And a loan shark, I think," said Sophie, not able to meet anyone's eyes. "I had no idea his gambling had gotten so out of control, until he just disappeared."

"Hmmm. And do you think if you tried to contact him he would respond?" asked Martin.

"I have absolutely no idea. He hasn't so far, but I can always try again."

Robert's chest felt tight at the thought of Damien having anything to do with Sophie again. As much as he needed to talk to his brother, he wasn't sure he'd be able to handle Damien tainting his girl any further.

Hold up, did I just think of her as my *girl?*

He sighed and rubbed his hand roughly through his hair again. Nothing was simple any more.

CHAPTER 16

It had been four weeks now since Sophie had left Sydney, and she had yet to properly discuss with Robert what the timeline was for her going back. She was loath to bring it up when they were so blissfully happy. Surely real life could wait a little longer?

Even after all this time, she hadn't acclimatized to the scorching heat of the outback. It was two o'clock in the afternoon and she donned a large, beaten-up cowboy hat, took a gulp of air-conditioned air and then stepped out onto the verandah. The heat actually *slapped* her in the face and she could feel her skin tightening in response to the temperature.

She'd left a hose soaking one end of the vegetable garden, which was shaded by a large Claret Ash tree, and wanted to move it to the other end. It seemed an impossible job to keep the moisture up in weather like this, but nevertheless she trudged across the lawn – even as the heat drained her energy and left her lethargic.

The dry lawn crunched under her feet and she thought briefly about turning some sprinklers on, but at this time of the day most of the water would just evaporate. Better to wait until it cooled down in the evening.

It was too hot for Robert to be doing any work out on the farm, instead he was in one of the sheds, going over the machinery that would be needed to start sowing the coming season's crops. Even being out of the direct heat, Sophie knew he'd soon come back to the house for a few hours to escape the temperature, and then head back out in the late afternoon to check on stock.

The air was still, with no breeze to offer a reprieve. Sophie noticed suddenly the unnatural quiet, and paused with the hose in her hands. At first, after leaving the hustle of the city, she thought life on the farm had been unbearably quiet. And then she became aware of the quiet sounds of rural life; melodious magpies and chuckling kookaburras, the air moving through the leaves of the Ghost Gums, the buzz of crickets in the evening.

Now these sounds were the unobtrusive background to her new life, and Sophie felt a tingle of fear at their sudden absence. The air was charged, and she wondered if Robert had forgotten to warn her there would be a thunderstorm today.

Dropping the hose into its new spot she turned towards the machinery sheds, grouped just beyond the house paddock, contemplating whether she should walk over there to check with Robert.

Her heart stopped in her chest.

Just for a beat, but in that missing beat she felt a world of terror yawn open before her. An enormous, cloudy red wall loomed – obscuring the whole horizon beyond the sheds, which appeared tiny in comparison to the oncoming force.

Sophie couldn't move; she wasn't sure whether to run towards Robert at the sheds, or back into the safety of the house. Was it smoke? Was there a bushfire? She couldn't smell a fire, and surely it wouldn't be that roiling, red brown colour?

She'd seen enough Hollywood blockbusters depicting a

dramatic Armageddon to half consider the end of the world was approaching. In which case, she wasn't cowering in the house and leaving Robert out in the elements by himself. She couldn't judge the distance between the massive swelling wall and herself; she just knew with a galvanizing urgency that she needed to get to Robert.

Already panting in the dry heat, she dashed towards the gate and out into the paddock. Her hat swept from her head with a sudden uplift of wind, which swept over the landscape with a vengeance, gusting up fallen branches and tearing through the trees, causing them to toss their leaves.

Millions of small particles of dirt stung her face, and she saw with rising dread that visibility had decreased in the time it took her to run three steps. Instinctively, she raised the hem of her t-shirt to cover her mouth and nose.

"Sophie! Jesus! What are you doing out here? Get back to the house!" Robert's voice bellowed out of the dust, followed by the outline of his body sprinting towards her. Raising an arm to shield her face, she stood buffeted by the violent wind, squinting her eyes, as he advanced on her.

"Run Sophie! Don't wait for me, get back to the house!"

She only just heard his voice over the roar of nature; stumbling a little, she turned back to the homestead and ran as hard as she could. In seconds, Robert had caught up to her and ran with her, throwing the shirt he'd been holding to his face over her instead, urging her forward.

As they sped through the gate into the backyard Sophie hazarded a glance backwards and halted dead at the sight of the rapidly advancing wall of dust and debris – it was frightening in in its sheer enormity. Jerking her by the arm, Robert pulled her onwards, picking her up in his arms to bound up the verandah steps. The farm cat was agitatedly mewing at the back door, desperate to get to safety.

"Fine, you can come in too," Robert growled, kicking the door open with Sophie still in his arms, the cat streaking past them. Breathless, they stood behind the closed door and just looked at each other. Robert's hair was beyond messy, dirt streaked his face and a fine coating of dust covered him from head to foot.

"Do I look as bad as you?" She screwed up her nose letting out a giggle. The giggle turned slightly hysterical. "I think I'm in shock. What the hell was that?"

Robert strode into the kitchen and deposited her gently onto a chair, before hunkering down in front of her and wiping his finger along her cheek.

"That, my little kitten, is a dust storm. And it arrived with absolutely no warning. I'm just going to get onto the two-way to let Wilko know it's coming his way."

Sophie heard their neighbour's voice cracking over the radio; "Thanks mate, I can see it rolling in. All good over your way?"

"Not sure, she's not fully passed us yet. The wind must be at least 60-kilometers an hour. Touch base when you're all clear. Over and out."

The interior of the house was dark and gloomy as the storm rushed over them; Sophie had had no reason to have the lights on when she'd headed out to the garden. Now, she stood to turn on the kitchen light, only to have it flicker and go out.

"Storm will be playing havoc with the power lines," Robert explained, coming to stand in front of her. "Come here babe." He pulled her to her feet and into his crushing embrace. "What on earth were you doing coming out to the shed? You should have been in the house."

"I was just out watering when I saw it coming, I had no idea what it was. Everything was so still, and then all of a sudden the wind picked up and it was right there." She shivered in his embrace, cold even though the air-conditioner had shut down with the electricity. "God, that was so scary. How long will it last?"

"The worst of it has probably just gone over us. But there's going to be a hell of a clean up job ahead now."

"What do you mean? Won't the dust just have blown away?"

"The wind is bound to have put tree branches down over fences, and I'll have to make sure the stock are okay and clean out all the water troughs. And you're not going to believe the amount of dirt that's going to be heaped over everything – we'll be cleaning dust out of nooks and crannies for months to come."

Hmmmm, months huh?

Sophie was highly interested in Robert's assuming she would still be here months into the future. Dare she hope he wasn't going to be satisfied with a fling either? Because dirt or no dirt, there was absolutely nowhere else she'd rather be than right here with him.

———

Steam was already filling the bathroom when Robert entered, having turned off the garden hose and confirmed with Wilko that he'd also come through unscathed.

It had been years since the last big dust storm had swept through the district, and the current drought conditions meant there had been plenty of topsoil just ready and waiting to be swept away. They *really* needed some rain in the next few weeks before they started sowing, otherwise the situation for this season's crops looked dire.

All thoughts of farming rapidly dissolved when he spotted Sophie's svelte form behind the opaque shower wall, bending down soaping her long legs.

Oh yeah.

He stripped off his clothes without taking his eyes off her alluring shadow, caring absolutely no fucks where the dust from his clothes and body were going. They could clean the room later. Right now, he wanted to clean their bodies.

Needed to clean their bodies.

The only immediate danger to Sophie outside had been eye irritation or the chance of being hit by something tossed around in the wind, but even knowing that, Robert had panicked when he'd seen her out there.

Now, he needed her close and his hands all over her body, just to reassure himself she was here, and she was fine.

Long showers were a rarity for Robert; with the homestead relying on rainwater – either caught in tanks or pumped from a nearby dam – the luxury of spending excess time in the shower just didn't exist. Today, however, he didn't care if the tanks ran dry.

Stepping into the shower he moved in behind Sophie and wrapped his arms around her, head dropping to rest on her shoulder as the water stream jetted over them both.

"I was clean, and now you've made me filthy again," she accused, turning in his arms to face him. "So I think you're obliged to wash me again."

"With pleasure," he said gruffly, running his hands up her arms and cupping the weight of her breasts in his hands.

She laughed, watching his hand track streaks of dirt across her body, the rivulets of water running off him the same red brown of the earth outside.

"Maybe I better clean you off first, huh?" and she moved to position him directly under the water spray. He tipped his head back, running his fingers through his hair to help the water dislodge the dirt. His eyes closed as he reveled in the sensation of the pummeling water and Sophie's hands moving over his body, scrubbing every inch of his bare skin.

He opened his eyes to find her in front of him again, lathering more soap between her hands and then, maintaining eye contact with him, lowering herself to her knees.

Oh my god yes.

Her hands firmly grasped his erection and ran up and down, dipping around to cup his balls. A groan tore itself from his throat as he leant forward to brace one hand against the shower wall, the other hand curving down around her nape.

Needing no further encouragement she brought his cock to her mouth, sliding her pink tongue right to the base, and then twirling it back up, all the while her eyes were locked on his. She smiled up at him and then closed her eyes to concentrate, one hand still cupping his balls and the other – fingers spread wide – on his abdomen.

His breath hitched as she sucked his length into the warmth of her mouth, the suction delicious. Up and down she bobbed, swallowing him right to the back of her throat and then almost releasing him completely before enveloping him again. His neck tendons corded as he struggled to keep control, wanting to prolong this delicious torture as long as he could.

When her hand left his balls he almost begged for its return, until it clenched around the base of his cock and squeezed tight as she increased her tempo, driving that mouth of hers up and down. His stomach muscles clenched and he groaned a warning, "Babe, I'm close."

He expected her to draw back and allow him to pump his release into her hand, instead she held him tighter and sucked harder. With an animalistic groan he came in her mouth, shuddering, watching as she swallowed.

This woman has ruined me.

Running the washcloth all over Sophie's body, steam swirling around them, Robert hardened again. He couldn't get enough of this woman.

Yes, she was as sexy as hell, but she'd also become his favourite person to spend time with. He craved her company, not just her body. He caught himself wondering more and more frequently if she'd ever consider this kind of life, for real.

Could a city girl like her ever be happy living on a farm?

Sure, she was enjoying herself now, but life on the land was hard – even for those born to it. Was it even fair to offer her this kind of lifestyle?

"I think we're clean now Robert," she purred, glancing at his straining erection and giving him an impish grin. "Want to do something about that big boy?"

"Did you seriously just call my cock 'big boy'?"

"Got a problem with that?"

"Not at all kitten, not at all."

She reached down and cupped his balls again, rolling them in her palm and tonguing first one nipple, and then his other.

"Christ I love that."

"What, this?" she squeezed and massaged, simultaneously closing her teeth around a nipple.

He was losing his mind. He literally could not focus on anything except the sensation of her. "Yes, that."

She slid her hands around his neck and pulled him down to meet her lips. He plunged his tongue inside, tangling with hers. There was a hunger, a passion, between them, and he needed to be inside her.

Grabbing her ass he hauled her up his body, securing her legs around his hips and pushing her back against the shower wall. She was slick and wet and warm, but out of the direct spray of the water she shivered, goose bumps on her arms, her nipples pebbling even tighter.

"Are you ready for this babe?" His hands circling her waist held her above his throbbing cock, watching her face and waiting for her answer.

"Oh god yes. Please. Now."

Slowly, slowly he lowered her onto him, until he was sheathed to the hilt in her delicious warmth. Unmoving, he stared into her eyes.

"This is perfect. You are perfect," he said, wanting to stay in this moment forever, even as the primal urge to fuck hammered through his veins.

"Kiss me Rob."

Their mouths fused together, taking and giving, and still he kept from thrusting inside her. Until she bucked her hips impatiently, and he lost himself. Breaking the kiss he grasped her hips, lifting her up and slamming her down, transfixed with the way her gorgeous breasts bounced. Again, and again.

Loving the slow slide out and then the jolt of pure pleasure as he rammed home again. Her eyes were wild with want, her nails digging into the skin of his shoulders. When he went to lift her again, she clung tight with her thighs and ground her pelvis into him.

"Harder. Take me hard."

They were without a condom, and Robert couldn't believe the sensation of skin to skin. He knew he'd have to pull out before finishing, but the *feeling* of being in her without any barrier was blowing his mind.

Moving his hands to cup her firm ass he pulled her tighter against him holding her steady, before thrusting in and out – his rhythm fast and hard. Her breasts were pressing against his chest and her fingers pulling at his hair. The tension was building in her body, her legs clamping tighter and her eyes squeezing shut. And then her internal walls clenched and she was shuddering her orgasm in his arms, his name on her lips.

Swiftly he withdrew from her, convulsing with his own release, head buried in her neck.

"I *can not* walk after that," she said when she finally regained her breath. "Please tell me you'll carry me to the bed." Her kiss-swollen lips pouted up at him.

He grinned and, without putting her down, turned off the tap and stepped dripping from the shower, shaking droplets from his hair and grabbing two towels. Stopping at the foot of his bed, she slid languorously from his arms to the mattress where he covered her with a towel, wrapping the other low on his hips.

He adored the sight of her spread over his bed, flushed and sated, and wanted nothing more than to fall down beside her and pull her back against his chest, wrap his arms around her and fall asleep. But he had other responsibilities.

"Babe, as much as I want to get in there with you, I'm going to have get dressed and head back out. I need to check the livestock and their water supply before it gets dark."

She surprised him by sitting up, rubbing the towel over herself efficiently. "Okay, if you're going out, then I'm going out with you. You'll need some help, right?"

He ran a hand through his wet hair, shaking his head slightly in wonder; "You never cease to amaze me. Yes, I'd love you to ride shotgun. But you're probably going to get dirty again."

"Well you'll just have to wash me again, won't you?" she smiled wickedly.

CHAPTER 17

It was while heaving over the bathroom sink for a third morning in a row that Sophie had to finally admit the possibility she may be pregnant.

Despair wasn't a weighty enough word to describe how she felt. And the morning sickness, if that's what it was, was crippling. Her knees tried to fold beneath her; the vomiting had left her weak and shaky.

Feeling the urge to throw up flash hot and urgent through her again, she moaned and, clutching the sink, lowered her head. Strings of hair hung limply in her face and were possibility being coated in regurgitated toast – she didn't care.

She stayed bent over the sink for long moments, leaning her upper body weight on the vanity. She knew now why people threw up in toilets – it was because they didn't have the strength to remain standing. She would love to sink to the floor right now, but she wasn't sure if she'd ever get back up.

Thank god Robert had already left for the morning, and had yet to witness this new state of affairs.

Although he had to be wondering if something was going on; she'd been so goddamn tired the last couple of days, literally falling into bed of an evening and passing out from exhaustion. The most intimate they'd been lately was sleeping, his long body curved behind hers. This morning he'd left early without even waking her, and she'd caught him eyeing her over dinner last night and for the life of her she couldn't decipher the emotion on his face.

Did he suspect also? Or, without the sex, did he think their time together was over?

Sophie didn't know what to think. She felt immensely foolish for not having put two and two together earlier, not to mention the *incredible* stupidity of getting pregnant in the first place. She wasn't a silly teenager; she was a grown woman who liked to think she was responsible and careful.

Clearly not responsible and careful enough.

Who the hell had an unplanned pregnancy in this day and age?

God, what would her parents say?

Fate was cruel with irony, because this child had been conceived the night before her photography session with Lani's family, which was when she'd had her epiphany about wanting a family. Wanting a baby.

Be careful what you wish for.

This was definitely not the way Sophie had imagined it happening.

She pushed herself away from the sink and stood up straight. Her pale face looked back at her in the mirror as she wiped a wet washcloth over it. Scraping her hair back, she tied it in a messy bun on top of her head.

Okay. Time to face facts.

If she wasn't, by some miracle, pregnant, then she had some other kind of illness. Either way, she needed to see a doctor. Minnippi had a medical clinic that was only serviced with a doctor three days a week, any emergencies went straight to the local hospital or, if serious, to the next nearest hospital which was two hours away.

Sophie cringed inside at the thought of someone seeing her go into the medical clinic. And someone *would* see her. She already knew nothing went unnoticed in a small town. There was no way she was talking to Robert about this until she knew for sure, and she would die if he heard about her visiting a doctor from anyone but her.

Maybe instead of a doctor, she could do a home pregnancy test? That way she could be discrete and, if she were pregnant, she'd need to see an obstetrician in Carindal anyway. She knew from Lani the Minnippi doctor didn't offer pre-natal care. So potentially she could bypass any overly-interested Minnippi residents entirely.

Now it was a matter of obtaining a home pregnancy test. It wasn't like she could just waltz into the Minnippi supermarket; her face heated at the thought of going through the checkout. The first time she'd bought groceries the girl at the cash register had quizzed her about where she'd come from, commented on her jeans (she'd liked them), told her that Julie and Mitchell Fitz had just split up (whoever they were), inquired what she was planning on cooking with the snow peas and asked why on earth she was buying coconut oil, having not even realised the store stocked it.

Yep, so not buying a home pregnancy test there.

She could buy one online and have it posted, but that wasn't ideal… Mail was only delivered to the farm three times a week, and she'd have to stalk the postman to ensure she picked up the parcel and not Robert. And besides, she wasn't sure she could wait the time it would take to arrive.

She needed an excuse to drive to Carindal, preferably without Robert.

"I can appreciate you're busy Mr Harris, but I still haven't had a response from the email I sent last week," Sophie tried to keep her voice level as she spoke with the accounts department of her old job.

"I just want to know why I wasn't paid for my last month with the magazine, and to find out if I'm entitled to a pay out of annual leave."

Sitting at the kitchen bench, Sophie absently scribbled circles on the paper in front of her as she waited for the guy to check her record. She'd been putting off making the call because she hated any kind of confrontation, but after checking her bank account she didn't have a choice. She was desperately low on funds and the invoice she'd submitted for her recent freelance work wasn't going to be paid for another week.

She'd only managed to pay her mobile phone bill last week because in lieu of actual time or affection, her parents had given her cash for her recent birthday. Thanks Mummy and Daddy.

Mr Harris came back on the line; "It looks like you resigned with no notice, which is why your wage was put on hold."

"But you can't do that! I worked those weeks, I deserve to be paid."

"And you will be. But because your actions were outside of normal procedure, the system needs time to process."

"That's bullshit! You're just stalling on paying me."

"I can assure you that's not the case Miss Richards. And using foul language isn't going to help you."

Sophie took a deep breath. She was at a loss for words. All except the swearing variety, which obviously weren't going to assist in this situation. She needed that money, but she couldn't afford to piss off the person responsible for making it happen.

"Fine. Can you please call me back when you know when I can expect the money?"

"I can do that Miss Richards. Have a nice day." The call disconnected.

"Fuck!" she thumped her phone down on the bench. "Fuckity fuck."

"What's going on kitten?"

She jumped on the stool and spun around, almost losing her balance. "Jesus you scared me! I didn't realise you were home!"

He frowned and walked to the other side of the bench. "Do you need money?"

She just looked at him without answering. What did she say? She really didn't want him to know exactly how dire her financial position was, because she didn't want him to think she was only staying with him because she couldn't afford not to. Now that here was no danger in her being in Sydney, she could always crash on Sara's couch or, if it came to it, go home to her parents.

Kill me now.

No, she was still here because she couldn't bear to *not* be here.

But she needed to get her shit together because if she was growing a tiny human right now, she was going to need money. She'd had to scrounge through her wallet to ensure she had enough coins to purchase the pregnancy test, which thankfully she did. Now, she just had to buy the damn thing.

"I'm just finalizing things with the publishing company,

that's all. Tying up loose ends."

She'd aimed for a breezy reply, but Robert was still watching her with an inscrutable look on his face, his arms crossed over his chest. And he made no move to round the bench to get closer to her.

She missed his nearness. Ever since they'd started this *thing* together, they'd been unable to stop touching each other. Not just in a sexual way, but in an affectionate, easygoing manner that she'd never known before, but craved with all her heart.

And it was her heart that was the problem here. Oh yeah, and her uterus.

"Do you want a cup of tea?" Avoiding his stare, she hopped down from the stool and went to flick the kettle on, keeping her back to him as she grabbed two mugs. "I was wondering if it would be okay if I borrowed your ute to go into Carindal? I'm getting a bit bored and thought a change of scenery would be fun."

She didn't look at him as she busied herself making the tea. She was outright lying to him, and was so uncomfortable she couldn't bear to face him. Unable to stop herself, she continued in a rush; "I just thought it would be nice to have a look around, do something a bit different."

"I didn't know you were bored here. I'm sorry. The keys are hanging by the back door. I'll see you when you get back."

Scrunching her eyes up at her own words she spun back around to face him, already regretting her choice of excuse, but his broad back was rapidly retreating. Whatever he'd come back to the house for forgotten.

"Shit! That was the lamest excuse *ever*," she muttered to herself. It felt really crappy to have not just lied to him, but to have lied about her feelings associated with being here. The back of her neck was hot and prickly and a lump formed in her throat. She'd hurt him, and she knew it.

Maybe she could bring back takeaway Indian with her for their dinner tonight, to make it up to him. She hated him to think she was bored and she could kick herself for not coming up with a better reason.

Damn. But surely after a day away to alleviate her 'boredom' they could go back to normal. *Right?*

She dumped both untouched cups of tea down the sink. Now was not the time to worry about the troubling emotional distance between them. She needed to get to Carindal, because if she was pregnant with Robert's baby then funny looks from the man would be the least of her troubles.

———

Sophie's presence at the farm manifested itself in numerous small habits and one of the ways Robert liked best was when he strode into the backyard to see her fancy, lacy underwear hanging from the clothesline.

The wisps of fabric looked tiny and unsubstantial pegged all in a row, but he could look at each piece, picture it gracing her body, and have a raging hard on in an instant.

But right now, as he stalked from the house with her words ringing in his ears, they were the last things he wanted to lay eyes on.

"I'm getting a bit bored."

Five little words and his whole life had collapsed in on itself. His throat constricted and he swallowed hard. He'd thought this mess with Damien had spun his world. But this? This was tilting the whole thing off its axis.

His chest ached. He was shocked he hadn't realised how important Sophie had become to him. And she was getting ready to leave. He knew it. His heart was jackhammering and he fought to think clearly.

He needed to talk to her about this, find out what her reasons were to see if he could counter-argue them. He wasn't going to beg her to stay, but he at least wanted to have a conversation about it. What they had together deserved that much at least, didn't it?

Cursing under his breath he swung into the jeep and whistled for Rosie to jump up. The dog sat and cocked her head at him before bounding into the back tray. She could sense his diabolical mood and treading cautiously.

Obviously he knew that Damien had left her with money issues, but he hadn't actually asked her about it. How could he have been so stupid? Did she need money? He raged internally that she was asking someone else for it, and not him. He wanted to be the one to provide for her.

This emotional distance between them was killing him. But she was the one who hadn't been able to face him in the kitchen, and so he'd hesitated to address it. After all, they hadn't made any commitments to each other.

Anything but love, right?

He spent the next few hours distracted, driving around the paddocks checking water troughs and salt lick blocks. The mindless task wasn't doing anything to engage him. He couldn't get Sophie out of his head.

He knew that relationships mellowed and it was unrealistic to expect they would continue to have the amount of mind-blowing sex they'd started this fling with. Hell, he'd *never* had this amount of sex before, even of the average variety.

Sex with Sophie was a completely new experience – it transcended the actual physicality and became something more. What that more was, he didn't really want to think about.

It wasn't like he was falling in love with her or anything. He just really, *really* liked her. And he still really, really liked her without the sex. But it hadn't been a slow wind down; one afternoon she was going down on him in the shower, and then – nothing.

He was confused as hell.

Added to that, she'd been quieter than normal. Teasing her about her chatter was something he loved to do, but there was nothing to tease about now. She was withdrawing from him.

He lugged a replacement salt lick off the back of the ute and let it drop to the ground, absentmindedly watching some grey kangaroos bound up the fence line. The scarcer the feed became, the braver the wildlife were becoming at foraging into the paddocks during daylight hours.

He pushed his hat back on his head, eyes scanning the landscape. He wasn't sure when it had happened, but he'd begun to think of Sophie as a part of his life here on the farm. He liked having her around. No, he *loved* having her around. He hadn't realised just how lonely he'd been, living out here by himself. And he hated to think about the silence and the space that would be left when she did go.

He had a growing certainty that that time was coming sooner rather than later.

This morning she'd looked so sweet and vulnerable, cuddled up among the pillows. She actually slept with her cheek resting on her palm – like they do in mattress commercials on television – and he found it ridiculously cute. He didn't have the heart to wake her before he left, and now he really wished he had. If she wasn't going to be around much longer then he wanted to make the most of what time they did have.

As he got back into the ute his phone rang, a number he didn't know.

"Robert Dayleford."

"Mr Dayleford, it's good to speak to you. This is Cameron Mullins, from Mullins and Sons Property Agents."

Robert didn't speak; he didn't have anything to say. He just waited.

"Ah yes, well. This is a courtesy call to let you know I'm bringing a prospective buyer to look around Acacia Ridge. We'll be there at around 2.00pm tomorrow."

Robert clenched his teeth and still didn't speak, lowering his forehead to rest on the steering wheel. Fucking hell. He'd known it would come to this, and it seemed he was powerless to do anything to stop it. His chest tightened as he raised his head and looked over the land that had been in his family for generations.

Was he really about to lose it?

"Mr Dayleford? Are you still there?"

"I'm here. Tomorrow isn't a good time."

"Well when would be a good time? The family isn't from around this district and they've got to travel to get here. I don't want to inconvenience them."

"I'm sorry I'm *inconveniencing* them," snapped Robert.

"But you're going to have to tell them to put their plans on hold indefinitely. As far as I'm concerned, the property isn't for sale and the matter is in the hands of my lawyer. If you want to speak to someone, you can contact him."

Robert could hear the tap, tap tapping of something on Mullins' end of the phone and then he came back on. "Okay, would next Tuesday afternoon suit?"

Seriously, what the fuck?

"Are you not hearing me? The farm is not for sale. And you better not step one foot onto my land." It was gruff and curt, and Robert hung up straight afterwards, flooring the ute back down the fence line.

CHAPTER 18

Sophie took her time washing her hands at the bathroom sink, unable to raise her eyes to see herself in the mirror. The pregnancy test she'd just peed on sat inoffensively on the edge of the bathtub, not knowing it had the power to change her life.

Shit, shit, shit. Fuck. Shit, shit.

She wasn't sure what to do with herself while she waited for the result, but she did know she couldn't look at the test until the three minutes was up. She didn't want an early reading to give her a false result. Nope, she'd just have to occupy herself for these agonizing 180 seconds.

The drive to Carindal had been uneventful and she hadn't bothered to go anywhere but the pharmacy. She had considered ducking into the public toilets to do the test, just so she didn't have to suffer the uncertainty the whole way back home. But she'd decided that if she was pregnant, she didn't want to find out while sitting on the lid of a stinky public toilet, looking at the back of a graffitied door.

It didn't seem like the most auspicious start to a pregnancy.

And she'd ditched the idea of bringing home Indian takeaway because just the thought of the food's aroma made her gag; she'd never have made the trip home without throwing up. Plus, she'd had a strange urge to return to the farm as soon as she could. The place had grown on her more than she cared to admit.

She stilled as she heard Robert's footsteps outside the bathroom door. She was in the main bathroom and not his ensuite, which he probably found strange seeing as she'd basically moved into his room now.

"Soph, are you in there?"

His voice was quiet and he sounded tentative. She had to fight the urge to open the door and throw herself into his arms. She ached with missing him. Missing the easy intimacy they'd established. She had no idea how he would react if she were pregnant.

"I'll be out in a few minutes."

She placed her palms flat against the back of the door and rested her forehead against it, willing her heart rate to calm down.

"Don't rush. I just wanted to let you know that I'm heading out for another Rural Fire Service meeting. I don't know how late I'll be, so don't wait up."

"Oh, okay. Do you want me to keep some dinner in the oven for you?"

"No, they'll put a barbeque on there. Did you try and call Damien again?"

She hated talking to him through the door, it felt like a barrier that was symbolizing something else in their relationship.

"I completely forgot! I meant to call you, but the phone reception was so patchy between here and Carindal. He sent me a text saying he'd be in touch. When I replied asking what that meant I didn't get anything back."

She heard Robert's heavy sigh.

"But that's good news, right? At least he's started some kind of communication. I can try and text him again if you like?"

"Don't bother. He's playing this on his own terms, and won't reply unless he's good and ready. I just wish I could see him to talk some sense into him, damn him."

Robert's frustration was a tangible thing, and Sophie wished for the millionth time she could do something to fix this mess. She even felt a tiny measure of guilt because she'd been living the high life with Damien, drinking champagne and dancing on yachts that were paid for with borrowed money. It didn't matter that she hadn't realised how their lifestyle was funded, all that mattered was that now someone was trying to collect on that money, and Robert was the one getting hurt in the process.

"Okay. I'll see you in the morning then."

"Night."

She didn't remove her forehead from the door until she heard Robert's footsteps fade away.

It was time to face her future.

Taking a deep breath, she picked up the pregnancy test with shaky hands, forcing her eyes to focus on the result window. She wanted a baby, she truly did. But right now, with her life so unsettled and the pregnancy unplanned? Well, it was far from an ideal situation.

One stripe was negative, two stripes was positive.

Two stripes…There were two stripes. One was faint, but it was unmistakably there. She was pregnant with Robert's baby.

After wrapping the test in tissues and throwing it in the bin, Sophie had gone straight to the pantry for the jar of Nutella. She was now propped up in Robert's bed, spooning it into her mouth while her mind grappled with the fact she was going to be a mother.

Holy shit. She was going to be a mother. She was going to have a *baby*. A little person wholly dependent on her. How would she know what to do? Even as she thought that she sat up a little straighter and brought her hands to cradle her stomach. She would work it out. Of course she would, she wanted this baby, no matter the circumstances.

Because regardless of whether Robert wanted to be involved, and to what degree, Sophie was keeping the baby. She had nothing against abortion, and firmly believed it was every woman's right to have that choice, it was just something she couldn't do.

Setting the jar of Nutella aside she moved her hands in gentle rubbing motions; it was incredible to think of the changes happening inside her right now. She wondered how long it would be until she showed. She had no idea what was involved with a pregnancy; none of her friends were up to that stage in their life yet. The morning she'd spent at Lani and Henry's with Archie was the most time she'd ever spent in the company of a small child.

She needed to Google how long morning sickness lasted for. And when she could go for her first scan to see the baby. Should she be taking pregnancy multivitamins? And what should she expect as her body progressed through the pregnancy? For example, how long was her libido going to be MIA?

Sex hadn't ever been a major part of her life, but that was because she'd never had the kind of sex that she shared with Robert. That man made her crave his body to a degree that she'd almost be embarrassed about if she hadn't been so sure it was reciprocated.

And sex was obviously a driving force for Robert, because since they'd stopped he'd started to distance himself.

She could hardly blame him; after all, they'd both agreed this was just a fling. Neither of them had made a commitment to each other, and certainly not one as permanent as having a child together.

She rolled out of bed and padded to the kitchen to retrieve her laptop from the bench – now was as good a time as any to start reading up on this whole pregnancy gig. She was startled by a flash of ginger at the kitchen window, and laughed at her own jumpiness when she realised it was the farm cat sitting on the window ledge. He gazed at her mournfully and let out a pitiful meow.

Ever since the dust storm, the cat had been acquiring a taste for indoor living, with Sophie sneaking it in whenever Robert wasn't home.

"I know how you feel kitty. Want to come inside and keep me company?"

When she opened the back door he was at her feet in an instant, winding affectionately around her legs. Scooping him up, she headed back to the bedroom, her laptop under her other arm. Settling them both back onto the bed, she propped the laptop open on her knees and typed in 'sex drive during pregnancy'. Obviously not her most pressing concern, but she was curious…

"Right cat. According to this, after early pregnancy nausea, vomiting, and fatigue, some women find that the second trimester is much easier on them. I've ticked all those boxes, so I guess I just have to hang out another couple of weeks to hit this magical second trimester."

She clicked on another website. "Ooo, this looks good:

'has your sex drive kicked into high gear during pregnancy?'. Not yet, but I bloody hope it does soon."

The cat stretched out indolently and yawned. "Mmm, I guess you don't really care about that, do you?" She scratched him under his chin, and he started to knead the doona cover with his claws. "Careful! If you leave claw marks there's no way I can hide your being here from Robert. Go easy on the bed linen mister."

Looking back at the glowing laptop screen she groaned. Was she seriously worried about her sex drive? Talk about trying to distract herself from the real problem. What the hell was she going to say to Robert?

She clicked shut the laptop resolutely, putting it on the bedside table. Google wasn't going to be any help to her when it came to the hard questions. Best case scenario was that Robert was thrilled with the news, and they lived a Happily Ever After here on the farm, "Highly bloody unlikely," she sighed to the cat.

Robert had never expressed any desire to have a family – he'd never even said he wanted this relationship to be more than a fling. However, Sophie knew the kind of man he was, and she had no doubt he would help support the child, even if he didn't want to be involved in raising it. So she guessed she didn't need to worry about the financial side of raising a child.

"Oh bugger! What if he thinks I did this on purpose to get money from him?"

She closed her eyes in horror at the thought. Especially after he'd overheard her conversation about needing money, and she'd been the one to assure him that it wasn't the right time in her cycle to get pregnant.

Fuckity fuck.

It wasn't morning sickness that made her stomach turn, it was a rising dread of the knowledge she needed to tell Robert he was going to be a father, and she had absolutely no idea how he was going to react.

———

They were wrapping up the Rural Fire Service meeting, just putting together a roster of who was going to be on farm over the next few weekends. The weather forecast was hot with extreme high fire danger, and they needed to ensure there would be enough farmers around if a fire were to start.

Last Summer they'd had two fires on properties during harvest, started by combine harvesters catching on fire when a build up of chaff had combusted. It was a frightening reminder of how quickly flames would spread over dry paddocks; there was a very good reason the Rural Fire Service had regular meetings to ensure the water trucks were maintained and to organise training days.

"So Robert, that was pretty good feedback from the beef collective's PR mob," said Ken Monrow, coming up to him as the meeting concluded.

"I haven't heard from them mate, what feedback?"

"They sent an email through yesterday saying there were impressed with the photography that you'd sent them. They're talking about putting together a promotional calendar for the restaurants we supply to, and want the details of the photographer so they can talk about fees and copyright."

Phil Jones ambled over to join them, swigging from a bottle

of beer. "Are you two talking about the beef collective?" he cuffed Robert on the shoulder good naturedly, "what about them wanting to make you a calendar girl? They obviously haven't seen my mug, or you'd be replaced in a heartbeat."

"I'll have to check my email, I've been a bit preoccupied the last couple of days," said Robert.

"I'll bet you have mate! Is that city chick still staying with you?"

Phil's question was casual enough, but Robert didn't want to discuss Sophie with anyone. It had thrown him that she was using the main bathroom again, and he was sure it was another sign that she was going to be moving on soon. It was stupid of him to have gotten used to having her around when it was never going to be long-term.

It was a good thing she putting distance between them now, it would make it easier when she told him she was leaving.

With that depressing thought in mind, he said goodbye to his friends and neighbours and headed outside to his vehicle.

At this time of the evening it was always wise to be cautious driving on country roads, and tonight Robert was thankful he wasn't speeding when a mob of kangaroos burst through the scrub on the side of the road, bounding directly in front of him.

Swearing, he fought the impulse to slam on the brakes and swerve – which would most definitely have resulted in an accident – and instead took his foot off the accelerator and held steady with the steering wheel.

Through some miracle, none of the animals made contact

with his bull bar and disappeared safely over the fence on the other side of the road.

"Bloody hell, that could have been messy," he muttered, flicking his headlights in friendly warning as an oncoming car passed him.

He made a mental note to remind Sophie to keep a look out for wildlife if she was driving at night – not that he thought she'd try and leave at night, it's not like she had to sneak away. And she didn't even have a vehicle, which he hadn't thought of.

Maybe she felt trapped on the farm because she didn't have her own means of transport? He should have taken that lack of independence into consideration; it may be a contributing factor to why she was unhappy now.

He'd been single for so long he'd forgotten the effort that was involved in keeping a relationship happy and healthy. And what he had with Sophie was a relationship, he'd come to realise, and one that he wanted to keep. The possibility of a future together was worth the effort – he just needed to convince her of that too.

Acknowledging that, even to himself, was surprisingly liberating. All day his emotions had been swinging wildly, but now they calmed. He was grounded and sure of himself. Maybe a little nervous.

What if she didn't feel the same way?

He was sure that they could work out their lifestyle differences, and the knowledge he'd gained tonight about the beef collective boosted this confidence further – Sophie could build up a successful photography and freelance graphic design business that could be run from the farm.

Assuming she wants to stay...

Keeping a keen eye on the dark road ahead he took a quick glance at his watch; it wasn't too late – if Sophie was still awake when he got in he'd talk to her tonight. One way or another, he needed to know where he stood with her – especially in light of Damien finally getting in contact.

A trickle of unease slid down his back as the thought occurred to him that Sophie could choose to go back to Damien. They had been engaged to be married, after all. Maybe she knew he was coming back and that was the reason she was pulling away from him? Had she been using him this whole time, waiting until Damien returned?

He slammed his hand down on the steering wheel. No, he refused to believe that. What he had with Sophie was special, it meant something, and he knew she felt it too.

Pulling off his boots at the back door he entered the house, hoping against hope he'd find her in his bed, *their* bed, and not the guest bedroom.

The relief at seeing the bedside light on and her small form under the bedcovers was a physical thing. The tightness left his neck and he rolled his shoulders unconsciously, stopping in the doorway to assess if Sophie was sleeping.

Walking quietly closer a smile tugged at his lips. Damn if he didn't love the way she slept with her cheek resting on the palm of her hand. Her honey blonde hair was spread loosely over the pillow and her thick, inky lashes swept down onto her cheeks. He sat gently on the side of the bed and ran a finger lightly down the side of her face, marveling at the few tiny freckles that had appeared since she'd been at the farm.

He wanted to kiss each and every one of them, savouring

the intimacy of watching the woman he loved as she slept. Because he did, he realised.

He loved her.

His chest was tight, it was so full of love. He didn't just *feel* the love, he was *in* love. Madly. And so deeply it was kind of scaring the shit out of him, even as his whole body reveled in how perfect it felt.

In his wildest dreams he'd never thought it would be a woman like Sophie that he'd be sharing his future with. She'd grown up on pavements, not dirt. In a cityscape of bright lights, not the wide open spaces of his land. But no matter the differences, or maybe because of them, she was the only one for him. She'd captured his heart.

But it would have to wait for the morning for him to tell her, and hope like hell it would be enough to make her stay.

CHAPTER 19

Sophie had been awake for a little while, but didn't want to move in case she jinxed the fact that, for the first time in days, she wasn't feeling nauseous.

Experimentally, she stretched her legs, running them down the length of Robert's as she did so. He'd slept as he always did, wrapped around her from behind, cocooning her in the security of his strong arms.

Man did she love those arms.

And the scent of warm male in the early morning made her pulse quicken. He let out a complaining moan as she moved from those arms, but quieted when she turned to face him, running her hands lightly over his broad chest.

Yup, nausea was definitely *not* what she was feeling right now.

"Morning. I didn't hear you come in last night." She angled her head closer and pressed a kiss to his stubbled jaw, grinning when it scratched across her skin. There was nothing about this man she didn't like.

"Mmmm." Sleepily he pulled her closer, nestling her head onto his shoulder as he rested his chin on top. "The alarm hasn't even gone off yet. What are you doing awake?" he mumbled.

"I thought of a better way of waking you up," she replied cheekily, running her hands down his taut abdomen.

"Really?"

His voice was significantly more alert now and she could feel his cock stirring to life. "Really."

She wiggled down his body, nipping at his chest as she did so. His hands came up and held her still, sliding up her arms and into the hair at the nape of her neck, angling her head so he could capture her lips with his.

"Not that I don't like the idea of that kind of wake up call, because I do. But what I really need right now is you, here, right in front of me, where I can kiss this gorgeous face of yours."

Lucky I'm already lying down, because this man makes me dizzy.

Their tongues tangled languorously, there was no urgency, just a slow burning desire and a feeling of completeness. Until he cupped her breasts and she let out a sudden cry and pulled back sharply.

He jerked his hands back and looked down at her with wide eyes. "Babe! Whoa! What was that?"

She inched back from him and lowered her eyes, raising her hands to cover her swollen breasts, which were aching.

What was that? Holy hell her boobs hurt.

"Uh, nothing. I just... I guess that hurt?" she said uncertainly, still not meeting his eyes.

"Soph I'm so sorry. I didn't realise I was being rough."

She glanced up at him and, seeing his stricken face, looked away. He hadn't been rough at all, and ordinarily she'd have been urging him on. She just hadn't counted on her breasts being so tender.

Damn. Time to distract the man.

"I think it's time we went back to Plan A," she whispered seductively, running her tongue slowly along her bottom lip.

"Because I was really looking forward to that."

Not giving him a chance to respond, she shimmied down his body, lightly running her tightly budded nipples down his chest as she did so; just that slight sensation to their sensitive tips was enough to have her tingling all over. Pushing the sheet all the way down with her feet, she settled between his muscular thighs and sighed in pleasure.

She'd never considered a penis to be attractive before, but Robert's cock was damn near perfect. It strained upwards now, and she couldn't stop a quick grin as she slid her hands around and up it, caressing and teasing. Bracing herself with one hand on the mattress, the other took a firm grip at the base of his cock and she slowly sucked one of his balls into her mouth, rolling it gently before mirroring her actions on the other.

"Fuck! Soph!" Robert's thighs tightened and then contracted as he tried to control his reaction, his hands diving down to tangle in her hair. "That feels *incredible*."

Sophie hummed in agreement, her mouth full, and Robert's hands clenched in response. Looking up she could see his head thrown back on the pillow, his throat corded and his chest heaving. It was heady knowing she could have this affect on him, and she couldn't wait to make him come.

Laving his balls with her tongue one last time she turned her attention to his cock, pumping it with deliberate flicks of her wrist before engulfing it in her warm, wet and oh-so-willing mouth.

She lost count of time as she strung him out, using the heat and suction of her mouth to drive him crazy until, knowing he was close, she increased her tempo and was rewarded with a guttural groan and the hot stream of his release.

"Babe," he said after his breathing settled. "That was amazing. Seriously, best wake up call *ever*."

He was drowsy again, pulling her up to lie across his chest, lazily running his hands through her hair. She hoped she had reassured him; he thought he'd hurt her and it hadn't been fair to leave him believing that – the only other alternative was to explain why she was so sensitive, and she just wasn't ready to do that. She hadn't yet come up with the perfect way of telling him and she didn't want to rush it.

She couldn't risk it – there was too much at stake.

Considering the intimate things they'd done with each other, it was a false modesty to cover herself with his t-shirt as she rose from the bed and walked to the shower, but she couldn't help herself. Had he noticed her swollen breasts? Was her body already showing signs of the life it was growing? Closing the bathroom door behind her she sighed deeply.

She had to tell him, and soon.

Robert had been distant as they shared a quiet breakfast, and Sophie was oddly relieved when he headed out to the paddocks to check some fences and spray thistles. She knew he must be confused by her recent behavior, but until she was ready to tell him about the pregnancy there wasn't much she could do about it – even though the loss of relaxed familiarity between them saddened her. She missed it.

Throwing some bacon scraps out to the cat, she went to rinse their dishes before stacking them in the dishwasher. A knock at the back door startled her into almost dropping the mug she'd been holding. Carefully she set it on the counter, and then hastily pulled her still-damp hair into a messy bun, smoothing her hands down the too-big t-shirt of Robert's that she'd thrown on over her jeans.

She knew she looked slightly ridiculous wearing it, but it was soft with wear and had his musky male smell. She'd bottle that scent if she could.

Casual visitors weren't something that happened when you lived so far out of town, and she hadn't known they were expecting anyone. Although it must be someone they knew, as they'd gone to the back door and not the front one, which was rarely – if ever – used.

It was only after she swung the door open that she remembered the last time she'd opened the door on an unexpected visitor. You'd think after a visit from a violent thug she'd have learnt to check first.

Unfortunately not.

Damien stood before her, just as she remembered, and yet a complete stranger to her now. Had she really been prepared to marry this man? He still projected that arrogant confidence, although she finally saw the layer of smarminess beneath it, not quite disguised by his stylized good looks.

He was just as lean and his eyes were the same hue as Robert's, she realised with a start, although they lacked the depth she always saw in his brother's.

Did they look a bit wired? Was he on something?

She *did not* want to deal with him like this. There was a reason she'd ended things. Time apart had not softened the disappointment that coursed through her when she realised he was still using. She was so sick of feeling disappointed in him. By him. She'd loved this man once, and he hadn't loved her enough to try harder, to stop the gambling and the drugs.

"So you are here," he stated, eyes narrowing. "When I went back to the house and you weren't there I called Sara. She was quite pissed at me and wouldn't tell me where you were. Not until I said your safety was in jeopardy and I needed to see you urgently."

Sophie stared at him; she wasn't afraid of Damien, although she wished fervently Robert were here because she was feeling a little intimidated. And why the hell hadn't Sara called to let her know that Damien was trying to find her?

"What do you mean my safety is in jeopardy?" Sophie tried to still the tremble in her hands as she held fast to the doorframe. Instinctively she stepped back as Damien moved forwards trying to enter the house. Thinking better of it she squared up and continued to block the entry.

He smirked; "Oh, I just made that part up. I've sorted out that little misunderstanding about the money. What is interesting now, is that you're here shacked up with my brother."

He paused at the threshold and raised his eyebrows, "and it seems you're not going to allow me to enter my childhood home, which isn't very nice of you. The least you could do is welcome me home."

"You don't live here now Damien. And because of you, Robert probably won't for much longer either."

There was a meanness to Damien's smile. "Oh don't you worry your pretty little head about that. I told you, I sorted out that debt with Frankie and so I've decided there's no need to sell the farm. The lease payments from Robert come in quite useful."

"What? How could you come up with that kind of money? And where have you been?"

"I've been staying at Smiths' holiday house at Hervey Bay, working a few contacts in the sharemarket to clear up that annoying issue with Frankie. And imagine my surprise when I got back to Sydney heard you'd left. With my brother."

"Are you kidding? You emptied our bank account and left without a word, not returning any of my calls. And that 'annoying debt issue' was a little more serious than that. They sent a thug around to rough me up, looking for you! Do you have any idea how scared I was? Of what could have happened if Robert hadn't turned up?"

"Oh, so my big brother was the knight in shining armor was he? How chivalrous of him. It might be worth noting that because of the beating he gave Frankie's man, I had to cough up an extra ten grand. Remind me to thank him for that."

Sophie shook her head. She felt sick to the stomach knowing that she'd almost married this man. When had he become so damn horrible? She knew the drug taking had gradually distorted his personality even while she was with him, but this time apart from him only highlighted the change.

Seeing Damien now only cemented how right it felt with Robert – how important he had become to her. She loved him. Loved him like she'd never loved Damien.

"So why are you here then, if you're not selling the farm?"

"I came back for you, of course."

"You have *got* to be kidding!" she actually laughed, it was so ludicrous. She continued smiling at him, putting her hand to her heart and shaking her head in a parody of affection. "We're over Damien, and we've been over for months now. Whatever it is that you think we had together, it's nothing compared to what I have with Robert."

He mimicked her shaking head, but he wasn't smiling as

he stepped into her personal space. "We're not over Sophie, you need me. You need what I can give you. I gave you space when you broke off the engagement, knowing you'd reconsider. You're not going to stay out here in the sticks – I know how to make you happy."

Before she could grasp his intentions, he had grabbed her shoulders and forced his mouth down over hers, his tongue demanding entry. Gagging, she shoved at him hard but held her ground; she would not run from this man.

"You're disgusting. And I don't want anything to do with you. Get out of here, before Robert comes back."

"What is it he can give you that I can't? You're going to miss our lifestyle, you're not cut out for life in the bush," he hissed at her.

"I'm having his baby Damien," she said with quiet satisfaction, and without waiting for a response she turned and walked into the house, leaving him standing open mouthed in the door.

Standing in the bay windows at the front of the house she watched as Damien spun his tyres on the gravel driving away. Relief flooded her and she realised she didn't need a perfect way to tell Robert, she just had to tell him. She didn't need to be afraid to share this amazing news with him.

And oh god, had she just realised she was in love with Robert? The strength of her happiness made her giddy. Her head was actually spinning. She was wholly, completely, both boots in, madly in love. Euphoria bounced through her, exhilaration causing her heart to flutter madly and her cheeks to flush. Raising her hands to cup her face she sank onto the window seat, unable to think beyond this new, incredible realisation.

She was in love with Robert.

——

Robert was only a third of the way up the eastern fence line of the bore paddock when he remembered he hadn't told Sophie about the email from the PR company about her photography. He was proud on her behalf, and pulled his phone from his pocket to call her; he couldn't wait to hear the excited squeal he was betting she'd make.

When the call when straight to her message bank he shook his head indulgently – the woman was forever letting her phone run out of battery.

Disregarding the fact it was too early for smoko – and that he'd brought an esky full of food with him – he started back for the house. It was better he hadn't been able to call her, because he wanted to see her face when he told her the news. Maybe with the prospect of payment for her photography and knowing she wasn't completely reliant on him for money, she wouldn't feel funny about him buying a car for her.

And besides, they hadn't even had a chance yet to talk over Damien's text message, and what it could mean. Was that bloody stock and station agent still planning on bringing prospective buyers, and would Damien show too? If he thought witnesses were going to stop Robert giving him a bloody nose, then he thought wrong.

The thing of it was, Robert was fine with Damien owning half the farm. He was his brother, of course they should share the asset their parents had left them. And their arrangement for Robert to manage the farm and lease half from his brother was practical and had been amicable. What Robert couldn't stomach was the underhanded approach Damien was taking, and that he hadn't bothered to communicate to see if there were other options of working this thing out.

Didn't he have any idea of how much this land meant to Robert? Of how he'd poured everything he had into it to make it viable and successful?

As he drove he assessed the skyline, still no rain on the forecast. His vehicle was leaving billowing clouds of dust in its wake as he sped back towards Sophie. Maybe he should take the day off, and just spend it with her? He was worried about the exhaustion she didn't seem to be able to shake, and he was still feeling rattled from when he'd hurt her this morning.

Making the decision to call it quits for the day, he detoured via the dog kennel to put Rosie away, and happened to look up from over the fence at the back verandah. Which, even from this distance, gave him a perfect view of Sophie smiling that sweet smile of hers at his brother, before Damien stepped forward and kissed her.

The pain that blossomed in his chest assured him that yes, a heart *could* actually break, and his was now in pieces. Stunned, he reeled around so he no longer needed to see the embracing couple. He should have seen this coming. He'd been so stupid.

He knew Sophie had been pulling away and, with Damien so close to having money from the sale of the farm, she was obviously choosing to go back to him. Had he really thought she'd be happy with him, here on the farm?

Was he really so lonely that he could have fallen in love with a fling? A woman who'd never had any intention of staying?

Swinging back around, he barreled through the back gate toward them, a furious energy propelling him. Damien wanted to take the farm, and now he wanted to take Sophie too? Hell no.

He could live without the farm, if he had to. It would hurt, but he'd cope. Living without Sophie? That would kill him.

He believed in her, he believed in them. Now was the time to show her.

Blood was pounding so hard in Robert's head that he was deaf to everything. His single minded focus was on reaching the verandah, but even as he raced across the back lawn Damien was walking away, heading toward a car.

He was leaving?

Did he chase his brother, or stay to see Sophie? Hearing Damien's car start up galvanized Robert into action. Regardless of his all-consuming love for Sophie, he needed to see his brother. Sprinting back to his ute he tore down the driveway, squinting through the dust that Damien's car had blown up.

Swearing at the lack of visibility, he slowed the vehicle further, and in the millisecond between one blink and the next, several kangaroos were suddenly right in front of him. He felt the sickening crunch against the bull bar as it connected with the kangaroos, one of which was flung back up and straight against the windscreen, which shattered with an incredibly loud bang into an opaque mess of fractures.

His mind flashed. Was this going to be it? His life ended in a back road car accident just like his parents, before he'd had a chance to tell Sophie how he really felt?

No damn it!

Before he had a chance to react to the shock, another kangaroo from the mob also hurtled against the windscreen, this one breaking through the laminated glass. The injured animal was half inside the cabin with him, hissing and grunting as it's sharp-clawed paws scrabbled uselessly.

Robert completely lost control of the vehicle. His back tyres fishtailed on the gravel and he made the instinctive mistake of over-correcting, which sent the vehicle into a skid. Adrenalin surging, he fought to regain control while unable to see what was happening outside, until a dark shape loomed close and the vehicle slammed into a tree.

The airbag only partially deployed and Robert's chest slammed into the steering wheel with no buffer and his head slammed into the side window. He cried out in agony, a sudden and severe pain ripping through his chest.

"Oh god," Robert groaned into the sudden silence.

It had taken less than a minute from impact with the first kangaroo to where he was now – slumped over the steering wheel. The crash had caused the kangaroo in the windscreen to dislodge, leaving a gaping hole that was edged in blood and fur. Through it, he could see the bark of the tree, broken branches, and not much else.

The dust settled and the ticking over of the engine was the only sound. He hoped like hell the bloody thing wouldn't catch fire. To his relief he could move his arms and legs although the sharp pain in his chest was causing shortness of breath.

He shouldered the door open, which was wedged against scrubby roadside shrubs. The pain made him lightheaded.

Trying to catch his breath he leaned against the side of the vehicle, assessing the situation. He winced as he pressed his sides; he suspected he might have broken ribs, which could have resulted in a punctured lung – hence the chest pain. And the shortness of breath.

The hum of an approaching car grabbed his attention. He needed help and he wasn't sure how far off the road he was. If he'd crashed out of sight he'd need to get up onto the roadside to flag someone down. He felt in his pocket for his phone, which was thankfully still intact.

Without thinking, the first person he tried to call was Sophie, but again the call was directed straight to her message bank. Staggering around the back of the ute he realised he was in sight of the road and the oncoming car was slowing down.

"Robert! What the hell? Are you okay?" Damien leapt from his car and ran towards Robert.

"Hurts… to breathe. Ribs, and maybe lung."

Damien slung Robert's arm over his shoulder and half walked half dragged them away from the wrecked vehicle. "We need to get you to the hospital. Do you think you can ride with me, or do you want me to call an ambulance?"

"Quicker… if you take me."

Damien had to reach across Robert to help him do up his seatbelt, and Robert gritted his teeth at the close contact with his brother. It hurt his pride that he had to be rescued by him.

"Why did you… come… back for me?"

"I'm not a total asshole Robert. I saw you crash in my rear vision mirror. I wasn't going to just drive off and leave you there."

"Sophie. What were… you… doing with her?"

Damien glanced at him as he turned the car around. "Funny you ask that like you have a right. She's my fiancé, you know."

Hot anger blasted through Robert's synapses, eclipsing the searing pain he was in. He ground his teeth at the idea of Damien trying to claim Sophie. Over his dead body.

"Was."

"Right. My hero of a big brother has swept her off her feet." Damien couldn't hide his vengeful amusement. "Well I tell you what, this isn't all going to end bad for you. Sophie's coming back to Sydney with me, but I don't need to sell my share of the farm any more."

"You're not… selling… the farm?" And then, "What do you... mean... that Sophie is…going back to… Sydney?" Damn this breathless pain, he was struggling to pull a sentence together and the weakness in front of Damien was bitter. He swallowed hard, wincing as the pain in his chest stabbed resentfully.

"I was just heading into town while she packed. She didn't want me around while she told you she was leaving. But come on, you didn't really think that a girl like Sophie could stay living out here?"

Actually yeah, I'd thought she could. Had hoped she would.

That broken heart of his fractured further.

"Why should… I believe… a word you… say?" he demanded hoarsely. He loved this woman. And she hadn't told him she was leaving. Yet. He owed it to their relationship to give her the benefit of the doubt.

"You… don't have a great… track record… of telling the truth."

"Actually, that's where you're wrong big brother. I always tell the truth, because I don't particularly care when it hurts people. I was straight up with Sophie when she wanted me to change to save our relationship. It just wasn't something I was prepared to do. And even though she called it off then, she's reconsidered. And anyway, she needs to get back to Sydney."

"Why? Why does… she *need* to get back… to Sydney?"

"Because she can't arrange an abortion out here."

"What?!" Robert wondered if was going into shock. Had he heard correctly? He swung to face Damien's profile.

"Oh that's just precious. The baby daddy didn't even know," Damien sneered. "Well, well, she is a sneaky little one, isn't she? Sorry to spoil the secret."

Robert leant his head back against the headrest and closed his eyes. Sophie was pregnant? What. The. Hell?

Comprehension was a struggle. His breathing was labored and his chest hurt like hell. The pain made it difficult to concentrate on much more than drawing a breath in and easing it out.

They didn't speak for the rest of the trip to the hospital.

CHAPTER 20

Sophie needed to forget that Damien had kissed her. She'd already brushed her teeth and rinsed with mouthwash.

Twice.

She wondered idly why the touch of his mouth was so repulsive now, when mere months ago it had been such a normal thing. She'd known then that he used drugs recreationally but she couldn't remember feeling so repelled by him. Now, it made him unattractive and someone she didn't want to be with.

Had he been this bad before, and she'd just been too used to it to really notice?

She shuddered in disgust at herself. It was scary to think she'd nearly settled for Damien, and she'd never have known how real love could make you feel – shiny and light, safe and valued.

And besides, she had a few more important things to tell Robert, like that the farm was no longer for sale, and that she loved him. Oh, and that she was also carrying his baby. She was buoyed up from Damien's visit – she wasn't afraid of telling Robert about the pregnancy now – she knew what she wanted and she had to believe he'd be willing to take a chance on this amazing connection they had together.

It took her several minutes of rummaging to finally locate her phone, which was dead flat. No wonder she hadn't heard from Sara. Frustrated, she plugged it into the battery charger and tapped her fingers against it waiting for it to light up, before abandoning it and going to the two-way radio. She didn't feel she could wait the few minutes until the phone was ready to use, she needed to talk to Robert *now*.

"Are you on channel Robert?"

She let go of the button and waited, listening to the relentless static coming over the frequency.

"Robert, are you on channel?"

Still nothing. Damn.

She ran back to her phone, which still didn't have enough charge to make a call. She didn't know where this sudden sense of urgency had come from, but she was jittery with her need to make contact with Robert.

Fuck fuckity fuck.

She could take the old farm jeep out to see if she could find him in the bore paddock, but she wasn't totally confident in her navigational ability to find her way there – the farm was a big place.

She let a slow breath out and tried to remember some of her yoga breathing exercises.

Calm it down Soph.

She had a new design brief that had come through from one of the magazines yesterday, which she'd planned to get started on today but sitting down now she found she couldn't concentrate. Even searching for the perfect font to use, which normally she derived so much pleasure from, couldn't hold her attention.

She jumped up and flicked the kettle on, reasoning a cup of green tea would help clarify her thoughts.

The problem was, it wasn't her thoughts that were jumbled. It was just a weird *feeling* that coursed through her, making her jumpy and unsettled.

She paced the kitchen while the kettle boiled, which was taking far too long. Before it had whistled she had already tried the two-way again, with no response, and gone and got her phone off the charger.

While making the cup of tea she tried calling Robert. It rang and rang, and then his voice mail picked up, with his brief "leave a message, thanks".

"Robert, it's me. Sophie. Just wanted to talk. Call me back when you can. Bye."

As she hung up the two-way radio crackled to life. "Sophie, are you on channel?"

Even knowing it wasn't Robert's voice on the radio, Sophie grabbed at the handset like it was the last pair of size 10 Sass & Bide jeans in their warehouse clearance sale. "Yes! Hello?"

"Soph, it's Wilko. I just heard you trying to get Robert. Sorry love, but I just heard that Robert's been involved in an accident."

Sophie's legs went weak and her heart jumped into her throat, so much so she struggled to squeeze words past it.

"What accident?" she managed to strangle out.

Her euphoria from earlier settled as a cold, hard lump in her stomach. He had to be okay. He *had* to be. She had so much to tell him. They had so much ahead of them…

"The rescue crew are towing his ute away now, and Robert's been taken to the hospital. Ran into a mob of kangaroos."

"But he's okay?

"He's conscious, but I'm not sure what his injuries are. Do you need me to come and get you and take you into town?"

"Yes. Yes please. I'd really appreciate that Wilko."

"Okay. Hang on, and I'll be there in 10."

Stunned, Sophie looked at the radio handset for several moments before she pulled herself together. *Please let him be okay. Please.*

She'd never prayed before, but she was willing to fall to her knees now and beg. He *had* to be okay.

She was waiting at the front garden gate when Wilko pulled up, and jumped in with only the briefest greeting.

"He's going to be okay you know," Wilko assured her, driving the loop around the Claret Ash and then heading back out the driveway.

"Have you heard anything? Is he okay?"

"I haven't heard anything since I heard the rescue crew on the two-way, but I know that he was taken to the hospital by a passing motorist, and not in an ambulance, which has to be a good thing."

The drive into town was interminable to Sophie, who jiggered her legs impatiently and kept checking her half-charged phone.

"He didn't call you?" Wilko asked, noting her glancing at the phone for the hundredth time.

"I had two missed calls from him, but he hasn't answered when I've tried to call him back."

"He'll be okay, you'll see."

Sophie didn't have the strength to answer him. Until she saw Robert with her own eyes she couldn't help but imagine the worst. And it was tearing her apart.

As they drove through the hospital gates, Sophie was about to ask Wilko to drop her off at the front entrance doors while he found a park. But in seconds she realised the country hospital only had a small car park, which was mostly empty at that.

"Look, the ambulance is still in the dock. That means they haven't taken him anywhere," noted Wilko, pulling into a car spot next to the one reserved for the doctor, which was empty.

"The doctor's not even here! What does that mean?" Sophie fretted.

"He's not here full-time. Our nurses are top-notch though, they barely even need a doctor," Wilko reassured her.

Together they hurried through the front doors, Wilko pointing the way towards the accident department.

"Ah, you must be Sophie," brayed a surprisingly small nurse, given the size of her voice. "I've heard about you. I'm Shirley Reynolds, I'm assuming you're here to see Robert?"

"Where is he? Is he okay?"

"He's just with Suz in x-ray. He'll be back soon. We're just confirming it's not a traumatic pneumothorax, and want to see exactly how many ribs were broken."

Sophie didn't realise she'd swayed until Wilko steadied her; "See? I told you he'd be fine. I've broken ribs on the footy field before – nothing serious."

"Traumatic pneumothorax?" Sophie's voice was small. "What is that?"

"A fancy way of saying it could be a punctured lung. He'll live, don't worry." Noting Sophie's pale complexion, Nurse Reynolds hustled her into a room and sat her in a chair next to the empty hospital bed. "Just sit tight here love, he'll be back in a jiffy."

Wilko grinned at Sophie. "You look like you're going to puke. You going to be okay?" She nodded weakly. "Righto. Well I'm going to leave you to it. I've got a b-double arriving with fertilizer that they're going to need help with auguring into the field bin, so I've gotta get going."

"Thanks so much Wilko, really. I don't know what I would have done without you."

"Anytime angel," and with a wink he was gone.

———

Robert thought it unnecessary to be put into a wheelchair to go back to his room. He hadn't punctured a lung and even with the chest pain, he could still walk. But Suz was a stickler for procedure and he suspected she quite liked having big burly blokes at her mercy.

She'd finished school the year after him and so ran in the same social circles, which meant she'd heard all about Sophie's arrival.

"Your brother didn't stay long after you'd been admitted," she commented archly, hoping to bait him into conversation.

"Just drop it Suz. I don't know where he's gone, and I don't care either."

"Hmmm, touchy one, huh?"

"Seriously Suz, knock it off. And how about some more pain relief?"

Through his fog of pain he wasn't paying too much attention as Suz wheeled him into his room, and only noticed Sophie's presence when Suz abruptly stopped and then started giving him instructions in a faux-clinical, professional manner – at odds to the personal grilling he'd been enduring from her for the past 20 minutes.

Sophie stood and he noted how pale she looked but he

couldn't stand to look at her directly. Neither of them spoke, allowing Suz to control the situation and get Robert settled back into the bed.

"The doctor is on his way, and he'll check you over," Suz said, flipping through his notes before putting them at the foot of the bed. "We'll want to keep you in for a couple of days to monitor your pain and keep on eye on you – you took a fairly hard knock to your head."

With her back to Sophie she raised her eyebrows comically at Robert and waggled them mischievously, before continuing efficiently, "Ring the bell if breathing becomes hard, and I'll top up your pain meds."

She exited, leaving silence in her wake.

Sophie moved to take his hand and he removed it from her reach. Ignoring her wounded look he asked instead, "Why are you here?"

His tone was hard and he could tell he'd hurt her. He bet it didn't feel as bad as your heart being ripped out, which is how he'd felt witnessing that intimate moment between her and Damien. And then learning from *his brother* that she was carrying his baby.

"What do you mean? Wilko told me about the accident and came and got me. I needed to know you were okay."

"Before you left with Damien?"

"Wha – what? How did you know he was here? I thought he hadn't seen you?" He could see the confusion in her eyes.

Jesus, even now, when she was leaving, she wasn't going to be straight with him. Not about Damien, and obviously not about the pregnancy.

"I saw you together."

"What do you mean?"

"I mean I saw you. Together. And I know you're going back with him."

His words were biting and his tone sharp. He pushed all feelings he had for her way, way back inside him and stomped on them for good measure.

If she was carrying *his baby*, and could even *consider* getting rid of it without letting him know, then she wasn't who he'd thought she was. Not even close. The pain of her betrayal slashed through him. The sooner he got over her, and out of this hospital, the sooner he could move on with his life and forget this whole sorry chapter of it.

He wouldn't make this mistake again. He'd been right before – when it came to a partner, he needed a born-and-bred country girl who was steady and capable. He didn't need fireworks. He didn't need passion. And the harsher he was with Sophie now, the sooner she'd leave.

"Robert Dayleford?"

Two police officers he didn't recognise stood at the door of his hospital room. "I'm Detective Carlon, and this is Officer Davis. Mind if we have a moment of your time?"

Robert guessed he'd been expecting the police to turn up – it had been an accident on a public road, after all. So he was surprised when they asked him the whereabouts of his brother. "Damien? I haven't seen him since he dropped me off here."

"Do you know where he might have gone?"

"Well he was on his way back out to the farm, to get her," his eyes slid to Sophie, who was sitting bolt upright in the chair.

"Ma'am? Do you know where he would be right now?"

"I have no idea. Why are you looking for him?"

"That's confidential information, I'm sorry."

"Well Robert's his brother and I was his fiancé. Surely we have a right to know why the police are looking for him?"

The policemen had some sort of silent eye conversation with each other, before the smaller one nodded. "He's wanted for alleged insider trading. We believe he conspired to cash in on confidential information, betting on the sharemarket."

"He did say that," Sophie breathed, almost to herself, and jumped when Detective Carlon pounced on her words.

"You knew what he was doing?"

"No! No. He just said when I saw him this morning that he'd been in Hervey Bay, staying at a friend's holiday house, and that he'd been working contacts in the sharemarket. He had a debt – with some guy called Frankie – that he needed to pay off urgently."

All three men in the room were eyeing her, the policemen assessing and Robert condemning.

"That would be Frankie Orazio, who's mixed up with the Rinaudo family," said Detective Carlon. "Ma'am, we're going to need to talk to you further. Can you accompany us to the station?"

"What, now? I just got here. I want to stay to make sure Robert is okay."

"I'm fine, I don't need you here Sophie."

Robert hardened his heart as Sophie crumpled under those words. He had to start thinking of himself first. She didn't know it, but this woman had turned his whole life upside down and inside out. He was disgusted that she hadn't told him about the baby. And hurt. So damn hurt. That betrayal hurt more than any broken rib could.

Suz, who Robert suspected had been loitering at the door,

bustled in at that moment and ordered everyone to leave, insisting her patient needed rest. As Sophie left with the policemen Robert reminded himself he was glad to see her gone, it wasn't any concern of his how she was feeling right now.

Out of sight, out of mind, he told himself firmly.

CHAPTER 21

Officer Davis dropped her back to the hospital after she'd been questioned for over two hours. As they were finishing the interview, they'd received a radio call that Damien had been sighted booking a room at The Royal Hotel and they were heading over to apprehend him.

Sophie dropped onto the bench outside the front doors, she couldn't face going inside just yet. She needed to process the day's events.

She felt hollow about Damien; any strong emotion related to him had vanished – she just didn't have it in her to rage against him. To blame him. No room even for confusion.

She did feel a vague concern about what would happen to him now, but it felt removed – like he was an old acquaintance she'd read about in a newspaper. Apparently he'd used confidential, price-sensitive information to bet on shifts in share prices – the specifics of his actions went way beyond Sophie's comprehension and the police had been quick to realise this.

She'd been able to give them details about some of his movements and contacts, and to verify certain dates, but apart from that hadn't proved useful to their investigation.

She was tired. Bone achingly tired. And sitting here alone, on a bench outside the hospital, she was close to tears. Robert had been closed off, even mean, when she'd seen him after the accident. She couldn't understand why Damien's arrival had upset him so much, and why that had affected their relationship. If he had seen Damien try to kiss her, he'd know she had pushed him away. And why on earth would he think she was leaving?

Right now she wanted nothing more than to curl up on that hospital bed with him – she craved the reassurance he really was going to be okay. That panicky desperation she'd endured as Wilko had driven her to the hospital hadn't fully subsided, and she needed to be near him. To see him. Touch him. Breathe him in. Through his hospital gown she'd glimpsed the angry bruises blooming across his chest and her heart hurt for him. Her heart hurt for her.

If only Damien had talked to Robert at the farm. Robert wouldn't have chased after him, wouldn't have hit those kangaroos. Better yet, Damien could have just called to let them know the property was off the market, and Robert and Sophie would have been at home right now, celebrating.

"Angel! What are you doing sitting out here?" Wilko stood in front of her shading his eyes from the sun with his hand. "I've been looking for you – I was about to come and bail you out of the cop shop. Michelle pointed out that with Robert's ute wrecked you'd be without a car. So she's going to drop her little car off here for you to use for a couple of days."

Sophie didn't know what to say, the thoughtfulness and generosity were beyond anything she'd expected and her throat clogged with tears. "Wilko, I can't let her do that. It's such a kind offer, but what will she do without a car?"

"She'll come out to the farm with me for a few days. Trust me, she's been looking a reason to shack up with me for ages," his grin was cheerful. "I'll probably never get her to leave!"

"But she hardly even knows me, I can't believe she even thought about what I'd need, let alone offer me her car."

"Out here we look after our own and you, Angel, are one of us. Of course we're going to look out for you, especially now when Robert is laid up. By the way, he's in a foul mood in there, I'm not surprised you're sitting out here instead of in there with him. But I'm pretty sure seeing your pretty face would cheer him up."

"I'm not so sure about that," said Sophie glumly. "It's all a bit of a mess right now."

"I'm guessing that has something to do with Damien turning up?"

The surprising kindness from a virtual stranger was Sophie's undoing, and a tear slid down her cheek. She didn't even try and wipe it away; everything just felt hopeless at the moment.

"Oh Angel, it's not all bad," said Wilko, sitting beside her and slinging an arm around her shoulder affectionately. "Robert will be back on his feet in no time. And what about the PR agency wanting to pay you copyright fees for your photography? With the hype they're making I bet you can squeeze top dollar out of them."

"What?" When the hell had that happened? "I haven't heard anything from them since I sent through the proofs."

"They sent an email to the collective a couple of days ago, keen as mustard to use your photos and commission some more. Didn't Robert tell you about it? He copped a fair ribbing at the RFS meeting last night because they're talking about making a calendar from the shots of him – which is fucking hilarious. We'll still be calling him Calendar Girl when we're sucking soup through our dentures."

Sophie felt the bottom drop out of her world. Why hadn't Robert told her about this? This news was everything she'd been hoping for and more – it could be the launch of a new career for her – and he hadn't bothered to let her know?

Why would he keep it from her? Was it because he didn't want anything tying her here? He obviously didn't want her to stay, he was even pushing for her to leave with Damien he was that keen to see her gone.

She was gutted. Too shocked to even feel the utter devastation she knew was lurking, ready to descend the moment she was alone.

Oh god, was she going to have to move back in with her parents?

She didn't realise she'd covered her face with her hands until she heard Wilko greet Henry Mayberry. She lowered them slowly, gulping back emotions threatening to burst out of her in a great snotty mess.

She needed to keep her shit together.

"Mate! Congrats on the new arrival! I heard it was a pink one," exclaimed Wilko, jumping up to slap Henry on the back.

"The sweetest thing you've ever seen," said Henry proudly. "They've transferred Lani and the bub back here from Carindal Hospital; I just left Arch with Mum and Dad and was coming back to check on my girls."

"Henry that's amazing news, congratulations." Sophie got to her wobbly feet and was surprised when the normally reserved Henry grabbed her up in a hug.

"You have to come and meet her. Help Lani decide on a name – she can't make up her mind."

"Go ahead Angel. We'll leave Michelle's car in the car

park – it's a blue Holden Astra – and I'll drop the keys to the girls at the front desk. Give me a call if you need anything," Wilko said before ambling off.

Henry's enthusiasm swept Sophie into the maternity ward where a tired but glowing Lani was propped up in bed, cradling the tiniest bundle of baby Sophie had ever seen.

"Oh Lani!" she breathed, coming to a cautious stop beside the bed and gazing in wonder at the sleeping babe, "she's gorgeous."

"Isn't she just? Wee little thing kept me up all last night, and I had to go into theatre to get the placenta removed, but she's just perfect."

"Surgery to remove the placenta?" Sophie *had not* come across this kind of detail in her Google searches.

"Ah, the joys of giving birth. I have so much to teach you," smiled Lani. "Seriously, before I had Archie all the mothers said labour would be fine, it was a bearable pain. They lied. It is fucking hideous, and it's my moral obligation to warn you."

"I don't know, everything looks pretty rosy right now," Sophie said hopefully.

"It's all worth it though, isn't it honey?" Henry was gazing adoringly at his wife and she laughed back at him.

"Easy for you to say big fella, you didn't push a baby out your hoo–ha and you don't have boobs the size of watermelons that could explode at any minute."

"And on that note, I think I'll leave you three for some bonding time," winked Henry. "Soph, which room is Robert in? I'll head on over there and give him some shit about reckless driving." Without waiting for an answer from Sophie he wandered out, jovially calling to one of the nurses to "look after my girls."

Lani and Sophie smiled at each other, and Lani settled back against the pillows. "Would you like to hold her?"

"Oh god no! I mean, she's beautiful, but I've never held a baby before – I'm not really sure how to do it." Sophie took a step back from the bed, just in case Lani thrust the baby into her unwilling arms.

"You won't break her, I promise. Babies are much more durable than you think. And you have to do it for the first time eventually, right?"

"Oh Lani!" the soft wail burst forth from Sophie and she collapsed onto the chair beside the bed. "I'm going to have to do it sooner than I ever thought – I'm pregnant."

"And is that good news or bad news?" Lani tentatively asked.

"Good! I think. I just – I haven't told Robert yet, and I'm not sure how he's going to take it. I thought everything between us was so great, but I'm getting the feeling that he's ready for me to move on – that he doesn't want me to stay."

"Do you love him?"

Sophie looked at Lani sadly, "I do. I do love him. But I don't think he loves me back."

"But you don't know he doesn't. Men are complicated when it comes to expressing their feelings, it goes back to their caveman beginnings – it's an underdeveloped skill. And if you're having his baby, then I think you have to take a chance, and straight up ask him. There's too much at stake to just walk away because you "think" he doesn't love you."

The baby mewled softly and then settled, rosebud lips pursed in what looked to be deep contemplation of this new world.

"You're right, I'm just scared. Because if he doesn't love

me, I have to face what my future is going to be without him, and as a single mother."

Tears clogged her throat again, but she didn't want to indulge in them here, not when they should be celebrating a new baby.

"I haven't even asked you her name. Henry said you were finding it hard to decide?"

"Claire. Our little Claire Bear. It was my Grandmother's name."

"It's perfect."

"You've got to be brave Soph, and fight for what you want. I think you and Robert make a beautiful couple, and I've seen how happy you make him. And I also have my own sneaky reasons for wanting you around – I need you to take some newborn photos of Claire for me."

Sophie laughed, "Of course, I'd be honoured."

"Good, then you better start getting used to her, and hold her."

With the afternoon sun infusing the hospital room with golden light, Sophie cradled Lani's sweet, milky-scented daughter. As one of Claire's tiny fists curled around Sophie's finger she marveled at the strength in the baby's cute dimpled hand, and her almost translucent mother of pearl fingernails.

The reality of her own pregnancy had never felt more right than as she sat there completely absorbed in the newborn.

"Hello Claire Bear. It's so nice to meet you."

———

The police had just called, letting Robert know that Damien

had been taken into custody. He didn't ask if Sophie had left the station. She'd made her choice to go back to Damien, and even though he couldn't stop the worry about what she'd now do – what with Damien in the lockup and all – he realised she didn't want him involved.

Bile rose in his throat every time he thought of her keeping the pregnancy from him; he was glad he hadn't had the chance to tell Sophie that he loved her – he could only imagine the panic and pity on her face.

He guessed she planned on using Damien's car to drive back to Sydney, and if he was ever going to feel grateful about sitting in hospital with a tube stuck in his chest, it was now – knowing that Sophie was probably back at Acacia Ridge, just about finished packing her bags. That was something he just couldn't stomach to watch.

He dozed for a while, and then jerked awake with a physical ache that had nothing to do with his injuries. He missed Sophie. The woman was, simply, amazing. And when he finally pieced his heart back together he'd work up some energy to be properly pissed at her. She was damn near perfect and without even knowing it had ruined him for any one else. No other woman was ever going to come close to her, to the connection he thought he'd felt between them.

He'd give anything to give his brother a swift kick up the backside right about now. He didn't deserve a second chance with Sophie and he had deep concerns about what she would do now – with Damien in jail, where would she turn? Obviously not back to him, maybe her friend Sara?

He shook his head and blew out a deep breath. Not his problem. She'd made that very clear when his brother had stuck his tongue down her throat.

"Fuck!" he growled in frustration and anger. And hurt.

"In a bit of pain there mate?" Henry strolled through the door, a sympathetic grimace on his face. "I've never broken ribs, but I hear they hurt like a bitch."

"Not a whole lot of fun," agreed Robert dryly. "What are you doing here?"

"Lani had the baby yesterday, she just got transferred back here. We've got ourselves a little girl."

"That's great news Henry, congratulations."

Although the fact Henry was welcoming a new baby, and Robert was losing an unborn one, wasn't lost on him. Those shattered shards of his heart pieced a little deeper.

"Sophie's in there with her now, they started getting into some details I'd rather not hear, so I thought I'd come and see how you're holding up."

Robert pushed himself up straighter in bed and then groaned when the movement caused sharp, jabbing pain. Why was Sophie at the hospital? He'd figured she'd be on her way back to Sydney now, and had fought the impulse to send her a text to watch out for kangaroos on the road.

Although I guess I gave her a pretty timely reminder today about watching out for wildlife on the road.

"Sophie's here? I thought she'd have left by now."

"She was sitting out the front with Wilko when I came in – I assumed she was on her way in to see you, but I guess she could have been about to head back out to the farm. Wilko said something about leaving Michelle's car for her to use."

"Why would Michelle let Sophie drive her car back to Sydney?"

"Sydney? No one said anything about Sydney," Henry was puzzled. "How hard was that knock to your head?"

"She's going back to Damien," said Robert flatly, letting his head fall back against the propped pillows. "I thought she would have left town by now."

"Well why did you let her go and do a stupid thing like that for? Anyone can see you two are crazy about each other."

"Not crazy enough, apparently."

"Robert, you can tell me to back off if you want, I get that this is between the two of you. But I feel like I need to tell you to man the fuck up. You love this woman, right?"

Robert refused to look at Henry, just stared at the ceiling and bunched the bed sheets in his fists. "What if I do?" he muttered.

"Well have you told her that? Because take it from me, women like Lani and Sophie don't come along every day. And you're a fucking idiot if you're going to let her walk away."

"She's made her choice."

And shattered me in the process.

"Well last I knew, your brother was in the slammer and Sophie is just down the hall getting clucky over my baby. So I'm not sure what choice you *think* she's made, but she's sure as hell not on her way back to Sydney. Seems to me like there's been a breakdown in communication somewhere along the line."

Robert finally met Henry's eyes and the two of them stared at each other in silence, which was broken as Shirley poked her head around the door, telling Robert she'd be in to check his vitals in a moment.

"You've got to take a chance on this one Robert, trust me," said Henry softly. "But like I said, none of my business. I'm going to head back to Lani, you take it easy here. And good luck."

Robert watched the door close behind him and punched his fists in the mattress. He was confused. And frightened. He couldn't remember the last time he'd been afraid, but he was now.

It scared the bejesus out of him to imagine living without Sophie.

Was he brave enough to face possible rejection? Did the fact that she was still here mean he had a chance?

Regardless, he had to see her one last time. She owed him a goodbye, if nothing else. Spurred on by this, he rang the bell for the nurse and hoped like hell that Sophie was still visiting with Lani.

"Hold your horses lad, I said I'd be back in a minute," grouched Shirley, entering the room.

"I need to see Sophie, I think she's in the maternity ward with Lani Mayberry. Do you think you could get her for me?"

Desperation obviously oozed from him, because Shirley's face softened somewhat and she clucked her tongue at him in a motherly fashion. "Visiting hours are over love, and I just told that girl of yours not to come back until tomorrow, you need your rest."

Undeterred, Robert was buoyed by this news; "So she was coming here, to see me?" Even he could hear the hope in his voice but he was unembarrassed, it felt like his whole world hinged on her answer.

"Had that glow women get after they've just held a newborn, and she was heading straight to you," the nurse smiled knowingly.

Robert fell back against the bed as he let out a victorious whoop. Clutching his chest against the pain he whispered, "Thank you baby Jesus."

CHAPTER 22

Sophie had had a restless nights sleep, lying awake listening to the sounds of the big house settling around her, the knowledge of how far she was from the next nearest human being a little frightening.

Since arriving at the farm all those weeks ago, she'd either had Robert's company in the house, or known he was somewhere on the property nearby.

Now, she felt very much alone.

She wondered how he was, if he was in much pain. God, she wished she'd been able to see him again yesterday afternoon.

The conversation with Lani kept circling in her head. She knew she owed it to herself, and their unborn baby, to speak to Robert and try and explain her feelings for him. She loved him, madly and completely, but she wasn't sure how to put that into words. She'd never felt like this before. How did you explain to someone that they owned your heart?

And what if he didn't feel the same way?

In no time at all, it seemed, her whole life had changed – priorities shifted. She'd gone from swanning around the city with a job on a prestigious magazine, her main concern being whether her spray tan was the exact shade, to living in the middle of nowhere trying to establish her own freelance business. She rarely wore makeup now and her numerous pairs of heels were gathering dust.

And she was happier than she'd ever been.

She couldn't care less if she never attended another party with fancy champagne and unpronounceable canapés. Her heart would be beyond content to wake up every morning to Robert's stubbled, sleepy face, and share a quiet coffee as they discussed the farm jobs for the day.

Fresh, handmade croissants from a local bakery were pretty much the only thing she could imagine that could make life more perfect.

That's what I miss about the city – the bakeries. And Queen Street deli and the seafood market. Oh, and Papa Mario's pizza...

With the thought of buttery pastry in mind she headed to the kitchen on a mission, she was pretty sure she'd seen dry yeast in the pantry. Visiting hours at the hospital weren't for another couple of hours, and she was determined to bring Robert croissants – didn't they say the way to a man's heart was through his stomach?

Sweeping her hair into a messy bun on top of her head she surveyed the pantry shelves, pulling down the ingredients before raiding the fridge for some more... Baking had always been relaxing for her, and as she methodically worked the flour into the butter, her mind finally quieted.

She created the soft dough then folded, rolled and folded again – soothed by the familiar actions. She cut and rolled the flat dough into triangles, and lightly brushed them with egg wash before leaving them to rise.

Dusting the flour from her hands she sighed happily; everything was going to be fine. And damn if she couldn't wait to eat these croissants.

Having put the pastries into the oven Sophie stood in front

of the full-length mirror in the bedroom, discarding outfit after outfit. She knew with absolute certainty that Robert wouldn't care what she was wearing, but even if he didn't know it yet – this was a big moment. And she wanted to be dressed accordingly.

She didn't want to dress like the city girl she'd been, but she was probably always going to over-dress for the occasion. She needed to stay true to her style while fitting into this new world. She'd fallen in love, not had a lobotomy – it was doubtful she'd be donning a fob chain any time soon.

She was debating a tailored chambray shirt over white jeans when she sniffed the air. Was that smoke?

Holy shit that was definitely smoke. The croissants! Spinning on her heel she dashed for the kitchen, just as the smoke alarm screeched it's warning, the shrill noise tearing through the house.

"Fuckfuckfuckfuckfuck!"

Bare feet slapping on the floorboards, she was so intent on reaching the kitchen that she burst from the hallway and ran smack into a very broad, firm chest.

"Easy kitten, I'm still a bit fragile."

Sophie felt the deep voice rumble out of the chest she was pressed against, and didn't know whether to laugh or cry. Clasping her upper arms gently, Robert set her back from him so he could look into her face, chuckling at her obvious distress.

"I'm assuming the rush is to save the charcoal I just pulled from the oven?"

"Oh god, are they completely ruined?"

"Considering I'm not sure what exactly they are, I'd say yes. Come on, we need to get that smoke detector off before we're both permanently deaf."

As they entered the smoky kitchen, they could hear heavy footsteps pounding up the verandah steps before a man Sophie had never seen burst into the room.

Wait, is he wearing an ambulance uniform?

Coming to a halt, Sophie could only watch as both men grabbed tea towels and began waving them beneath the shrieking alarm. Robert groaned in pain and immediately dropped his arm, although thankfully the noise stopped.

"Mate! What are you doing? Sit your ass down and stop doing anything strenuous," reprimanded the paramedic.

Eyes watering from the lingering smoke, Sophie looked between the two men in bewilderment. "Umm, What are you doing here, Robert? Shouldn't you still be in hospital?"

"Technically, yes. But I needed to see you, so Julian, our local ambo and all-round good bloke, offered to drive me out."

Ignoring Julian's repeated entreaties for him to sit down, Robert advanced on Sophie until he had crowded her against the kitchen wall, his eyes intent on rendering her speechless. The man was goddamn sex on legs. The effect his presence had on her was drugging; he just had to stare into her eyes and she was mush.

What croissants?

"I needed to see for myself you were still here," he said in a throaty whisper, reaching out a big hand to wipe a smudge of flour from her chin.

"Where else would I be?" she barely managed to get out. If he came any closer, chances are she would combust in an inferno of lust. It seemed the night without him had only heightened her awareness of his sheer, sexy masculinity.

Cupping his hands around her face, the calloused pads of his thumbs rubbed in gentle strokes up and down her heated cheeks. "I know you came back to see me yesterday. And it got me thinking about Damien and all the chaos and bullshit he's always pulling. And it made me think I needed to give you a chance to explain what was going on."

"There's *nothing* going on Robert. Nothing."

"I saw you with him."

"You already knew he came here and we talked."

His head lowered and he breathed into her parted mouth; "I mean seeing him kiss your lips. *My* lips." He moved closer still, until the softness of her body was pressed flush against his unyielding one.

"Sophie, I'm crazy about you and I'm willing to fight for you. To show you how much you mean to me. This stopped being a fling for me a long time ago, I'm only sorry that it took Damien coming here to get me to realise how much I want you. How much I need you."

Her breath was a soft pant and her eyes grew misty.

"I was never going to choose Damien over you. Ever. He kissed *me*, and you obviously didn't see me push him away two seconds later. I want you. I love you Robert."

She held her breath, her teeth biting down on her bottom lip. Was it too much too soon? The disastrous croissants, Julian, even her pregnancy, faded away until it was just this man in front of her; his reaction was *everything*.

"Oh god thank you!" he groaned, burying his face in her hair and clutching her close. Closing her eyes, Sophie gave herself up the brilliance of being ensconced in his arms, surrounded by his heat and smell and security.

"Okay Romeo, could you *please* take a seat?" groused

Julian. "I'll wait for you in the ambulance, but you need to take it easy. And we need to be back at the hospital before shift change, or we really will be in trouble and nurses are *not* the kind of people you want to piss off."

Reluctantly releasing Sophie, Robert moved over to the table and eased himself onto a bar stool, grimacing at Julian.

"Sorry, thanks for this. I know you're going out on a limb, and I don't want you to get caught up in red tape for helping me. I really do appreciate what you're doing."

Julian grinned; "Truth be told, it beats sitting around the hospital studying for my next accreditation. But just take it easy, you were in a pretty serious car accident less than 24 hours ago."

Recovering from her swoon, Sophie's desire quickly morphed to concern. "But he's okay, right?"

Julian was quick to reassure her. "He's going to be fine, they're just being cautious and want to monitor his pain levels. He'll be discharged in a day or two and then he's all yours – I hope you can control him better than the hospital can."

———

Julian headed back out to the ambulance, after making Robert promise he'd only be 10 minutes. They weren't exactly sneaking around, but it would definitely be preferable if none of the nursing staff discovered their little jaunt.

He owed Julian, big time.

He'd been desperate to see Sophie as soon as he could – he'd hardly slept last night and it wasn't just because he'd been kept awake by the sounds of the hospital and the nurses checking his vitals. It had more to do with his emotions veering wildly between hope and fear.

Fortunately Julian had stuck his head in to say hi, and together they'd plotted this morning's escapade.

He'd known he wasn't short of breath just because of the fractured ribs; it was a direct result of his anxiety over the possibility of losing Sophie.

And now, knowing that this incredible, amazing, sexy woman loved him, he felt like he was taking his first real breath in forever. The burst of oxygen through his body must have made him lightheaded, because watching Sophie watch him from across the kitchen was enough to make him dizzy.

That wild hope from last night had crystalised into pure joy when she'd told him nothing was going on.

She's not pregnant. She's not leaving with Damien.

His heart swelled in his chest. Love for her flooded his system – he didn't need to hold it in check any longer. Coming closer to him, she bit her lip, which was all kinds of adorable and did funny things to his gut.

Oh yeah, he loved this girl.

As he sat unmoving on the stool, she came to stand between his spread thighs, placing tentative hands on his shoulders.

"I don't want to hurt you," she murmured. "I didn't think about your injuries before..." her voice trailed off and she raised achingly tender eyes to his.

"Forget about that, I just need you in my arms."

Hands wrapped around her delectable hips, he tugged her closer until she was settled between his legs – just where he wanted her. The scent of her was heaven itself. He buried his head in her neck, one hand fisting silky hair that had tumbled loose, and the other holding the back of her neck with infinite care. His thumb rubbed gentle circles at her nape and he inhaled deeply, knowing as he did so that he couldn't live without this woman.

He pulled back, noting that her eyelids had fluttered closed and she was clutching his shoulders as though they were her anchors.

"Soph, what you said before – it means *everything*. You are everything to me. I love you so much it hurts."

His voice was low and throaty as his large hands framed her face, tilting her chin. Her eyes opened and he could see straight into her soul.

He needed to say this knowing that she heard, that she *felt*, every single word.

"I love you. I love you so damn much Sophie. I was afraid you didn't feel the same way, that you were having second thoughts about being here with me. And if I had just talked to you, told you how I felt, it would have solved so much angst. We need to promise that we'll always try to communicate – what we have is too precious to risk with misunderstanding and silences. Because you're it for me, this is a forever thing."

He stopped, surprised that baring his soul had been so easy and natural. Her cheeks were flushed and unshed tears brightened eyes that didn't waver from his own.

"I want forever with you too," she admitted tremulously, a small smile blossoming and making her glow. She linked her hands behind his neck, drawing his head forward so she could place the sweetest kiss on his lips.

They stayed like that, faces together and breathing each other in, for long minutes, until he sighed with regret and pulled back.

"I have to get back to the hospital. I'm surprised Julian isn't abusing the horn, telling me to get my butt back out there."

"That's okay, I'll finish getting ready and follow you. It'll be visiting hours by then. Do you need me to do anything here before I go?"

"It's all organised, I've got an extra farmhand starting this afternoon, to keep things on track while I'm less mobile. But thank you for thinking of it, you're going to make an excellent farm wife," he said with a wink.

Did I just say wife? Guess I did. I really like the sound of that.

"Wife huh?" she gave a giddy grin. And then turned to the charcoaled remains of her pastries, which he'd hastily thrown onto the sink when he'd pulled them from the smoking oven as he'd arrived.

"Lucky I don't need food to get to your heart, huh?" she quipped, dumping the blackened remains into the bin.

"Your cooking is just an added bonus," he grinned, before placing a lingering kiss on her lips. "I'll see you soon."

Robert shifted again in the hospital bed, the starched sheets rustling. He couldn't get comfortable and Shirley had given him the evil eye when she'd come on shift; she might not know about the earlier hijinks, but she definitely suspected something.

He was restless and craved Sophie. It was criminal that after declaring their feelings for each other, they were now denied each other's presence. Surely she wouldn't be too much longer?

As though on cue, the door to his room opened and she stepped through with a grin, looking back over her shoulder. "Did you get busted by Nurse Reynolds? She just gave me the filthiest look."

"Don't worry about Shirley and her filthy looks. You should be more concerned with my filthy thoughts," he promised, beckoning her closer.

Those long, long legs of hers were bare beneath that white sundress he loved so much. It was the same one she'd been slipping on that first day with her door wide open.

That had been a good day.

He was totally eye fucking her, and she knew it. Her lush lips parted and her tongue peeked out to swipe at her bottom lip in anticipation, before slowly starting towards him.

Hospital rooms should come with Do Not Disturb signs…

Despite her obvious excitement she sat primly on the side of his bed, mindful of his injuries, which was beyond frustrating. He needed her closer. He pressed the button to raise the head of his bed so he was upright, and then hauled her so she was sitting astride him.

She gasped. "Robert! Anyone could come in!"

"I don't give a damn."

Her hot center was directly above his already straining cock and he needed friction between them like he needed oxygen. Hands on her lower back he pressed her down onto him and the tiny moan that left her lips made all the blood in his body head south.

Smoothing his hands up her back he urged her forward. Those perfect nipples of hers were budded tightly beneath her dress, begging for his attention. He brought his eager mouth to them, breathing hot on them through the material as one hand snaked around to cup and knead her full breasts. She moaned out loud.

He loved the noises she made when aroused, but he sure as hell didn't want anyone else to hear. Sliding from beneath her he left the bed, dragging the visitors chair over to the door and jamming it beneath the handle, creating an effective lock.

"Now where were we?"

In seconds he had Sophie straddling him again, his lips on her throat, stubble grazing the sensitive skin.

"Mmmm, right about here," she whispered, grinding herself down onto him as his tongue licked into her mouth, their mutual need a pulsing demand.

As much as he longed to bury himself in her, he knew his injuries would make that difficult, if not impossible. Instead, he had to content himself with pleasuring her until shattering point.

No great hardship there.

She sat back, breathing heavily, and he ran his hands up her smooth thighs, bunching her dress around her waist. Pulling aside the lace of her panties, he ran a finger under. She was slick and swollen and he locked eyes with her as he slipped one finger and then two into her wetness. Eyes hooded, she ran her hands over her breasts, teasing and plucking her own nipples.

Hottest. Thing. Ever.

She rocked forward, her hands braced against the mattress either side of his head, giving him unfettered access to work his fingers inside her, increasing the tempo of his thrusts as she spurred him on.

Her responsiveness was possibly the most satisfying thing

he'd ever known and, appreciating she was on the cusp of orgasm, he pushed his fingers against her inner sweet spot.

Biting his neck she came hard and fast, her pleasure muffled against his skin. She slumped carefully against him, her chest still heaving, but stiffened immediately as a thumping knock echoed against the jammed door.

"Robert Dayleford! Open this door right this instant!"

"Impeccable timing Nurse Reynolds," Robert called back, "I think I need a cold shower."

CHAPTER 23

It was another day before Robert was discharged from hospital, and although Sophie spent every second of visiting hours with him, she *still* hadn't told him about the pregnancy.

It was eating her up inside, especially after Robert's heartfelt speech about communicating with each other. But every time she thought about telling him, the words stuck in her throat.

Literally.

Yesterday morning she'd actually choked and Robert had given her a funny look as he'd passed her a glass of water.

And she had a sneaky feeling she wasn't the only one keeping secrets. Robert had finally told her about the PR agency wanting to purchase the copyright for her photographs, but twice now she'd come into the room and he'd cut his phone conversation short. And both times his explanation had been unconvincing.

There was something he wasn't telling her.

She didn't know if it was her imagination or not, but she thought she'd detected a slight swell to her stomach this morning and her boobs had definitely gotten bigger and her nipples slightly darker. The minute Robert got her naked – which was likely the moment they stepped over the threshold at home – he would know. At the very least he'd suspect.

Like it or not, time wasn't on her side, and the longer she left telling him the more wrong it felt. Besides, she felt secure in their relationship now, she knew they had a future together.

So why was it so hard to tell him?

Mother Nature had finally relented and opened the skies, after an initial lashing storm the rain had settled into a steady, life-giving pour, which the parched earth absorbed gratefully.

Robert's insurance company had dropped off a replacement ute and it was from this that Sophie now alighted in the late afternoon gloom, heading into the hospital to pick him up.

Holding a jacket above her head in protection, she dashed towards the hospital entrance, unable to begrudge the downpour because she knew how much relief it was bringing to the region. Her steps quickened when she saw Robert waiting just within the front doors – he was obviously as impatient to get home as she was to have him there.

She entered in time to hear him telling a nurse that he didn't care if it was hospital procedure, he wasn't leaving in a wheelchair.

"We need to get out of here before they turn me into an invalid," he instructed, dipping his head for a brief kiss and then spinning her around, back to the door. "If I never eat green jelly again it'll be too soon. You know what I could eat? Some honey chicken from Little Dragon." He smacked his lips together in an exaggerated display of hunger.

"I have no idea what Little Dragon is," smiled Sophie, rolling her eyes in affection and making towards the driver's side of the ute.

"Not a chance kitten. I'm driving," he said firmly, opening the passenger door and gesturing for her to hop in. "And we're picking up some takeaway Chinese from Changpu –

he makes the best fried rice you've ever eaten."

They steamed up the windows of the ute with a serious make out session as they waited for their food to be ready, trickles of condensation were running down the window as Sophie watched Robert re-enter the restaurant to pick up their order. She wondered idly how tricky it would be to insert a "you're going to be a daddy" note into a fortune cookie, but was distracted as Robert turned around and winked at her.

Dear god he was divine.

"It's good to be home," Robert sighed in happiness, stretching his muscular legs out in front of him and rolling his shoulders to ease muscles that were tight from days of inactivity.

They were sitting across from each other on the lounge room's plush carpet, with the takeaway spread before them in an impromptu picnic on the coffee table. He eyed Sophie in amusement, watching as she devoured yet another helping of the Chinese. "You're hungry tonight. Looks like you're a convert to Changpu's fried rice too."

"Well I am eating for two," she said with fake nonchalance, watching his reaction from beneath lowered eyelashes as her heart jumped into her throat.

"What?" He stopped mid shoulder roll.

Her hands were trembling and her eyes were shiny.

Taking a deep breath, she pushed a paper napkin towards him, on which she'd hastily scrawled: You + Me = Three.

She waited one beat. Two. He was still staring at the napkin.

His eyes when he finally raised them were filled with tears, and a grin stretched slowly across those exquisitely chiseled cheeks of his.

"We're having a baby?" he whispered, reaching across the coffee table to grasp her wrists, bringing her hands up to cradle against his chest. "You're pregnant?"

She nodded, unable to speak with the emotion welling in her. This man was going to be the father of her baby, and his total acceptance and joy at the news made her heart full.

He jumped to his feet and rounded the coffee table so he could sweep her into a hug, lifting her from her feet as he swung her around.

"Oh Jesus, that hurts," he puffed, setting her back down. She made to step out of his embrace but he was quick to pull her back against him.

"We're having a baby," he repeated, in wonder. "I'm going to be a father."

"So it's good news, right?" She just needed to be absolutely certain, although his reaction so far made her feel slightly silly for asking.

"It's amazing news. The *best* news."

He dropped to his knees before her, placing large warm hands against her stomach. "You're growing my baby in there." He shook his head, "It's incredible."

She wound her hands into his hair and tugged his head to rest against her abdomen, soft tears falling down her face. All the worry and anxiety had dissolved, leaving her weightless and deliriously happy. Everything in her world was perfect; the excitement perfectly balanced by the contentment, the love for this man equaled by the joy of her new life out here – the one they'd be starting as a family together.

He tugged her down onto the floor with him and together they sat, his long legs and arms enveloping her as she snuggled against his chest. He was nuzzling his lips into her neck and his hot breath was doing delicious things to her body. Her breasts were heavy with desire and her nipples were aching for his touch. Her insides were melted… molten.

This man had her on fire.

"I might have already known."

She stilled, his words shooting ice through her system. "What do you mean?"

"Damien told me. He said that was why you were going back to Sydney, to get an abortion."

She gasped, shock and dread holding her immobile.

"But then when you said that nothing was going on, I thought he'd just made up the pregnancy to stir me up. That it wasn't true."

Sophie's stomach dropped. She'd already felt so awful for keeping the news from Robert for so long, and now for him to have heard it from Damien first…

"I would never have gotten rid of the baby – especially not without discussing it with you," she said hotly. "That is so not how I wanted to you find out," she whispered slowly, turning her head so she could see his expression.

"Hmmm, it wasn't ideal," he murmured into her neck. "I didn't realise how much I wanted it to be true – the pregnancy part, not the abortion, until you didn't say anything, and I thought you weren't. So now, for you to say it *is* true, well that's pretty fucking amazing."

She relaxed back against him, her heart beat resuming its normal rhythm as he twined his hands with hers and moved his lips up to her ear, nipping at the lobe and making her tremble.

"But if you feel like you need to make it up to me, I have

some ideas of how that could be achieved…"

Dear god she loved when his voice went all low and rumbly like that.

"And what would that involve exactly?" she purred, arching her back slightly and lifting their joined hands to run over her breasts.

"The removal of your jeans. And underwear. Actually, let's just take everything off."

His hands dropped to the zip of her jeans and hers began working open the buttons of her shirt – an action he couldn't tear his eyes away from as the smooth skin of her cleavage in a half-cup bra was revealed, button by button.

On his prompting, she lifted herself up so he could skim her jeans over her hips and down her legs, his hands caressing back up her calves and thighs, before helping her to shrug out of her shirt, leaving her captive before him in her sheer black lingerie.

"Maybe we won't take everything off just yet…" his gaze was appreciative and hungry, devouring the sight of her soft curves.

"Actually, I have something that goes with this, which I think you might like," and before he could protest she shimmied from his hold and got to her feet, hiding a secret smile as she headed for the bedroom. This lingerie set came with a French lace garter belt and stockings…

She had a brief surge of shyness as she came back to him – outfit complete with a pair of kick-ass black stilettos – but the heat that flared in Robert's gaze as he lounged on the couch quickly dispelled any nervousness.

He growled his approval, sitting forward, stalking her with his eyes as she sashayed toward him, putting a bit of extra sass into the sway of her hips.

This lingerie just justified its price tag. And then some.

"So, what can I do to make it up to you?" she asked with a quirk of her eyebrow, loving the way he was fixated on her tongue as it provocatively licked her bottom lip.

She was enjoying playing the vixen. Almost as much as he was.

Robert was too distracted in watching her to answer, so she dropped to her knees and ran her hands up his jean-clad thighs, breathing in his husky male scent, desperately wanting to taste him. Inhale him.

Her fingers started working at his button and zip, only to be stilled by his hand covering them. His mouth caught hers in a drugging kiss, sucking on her bottom lip.

"Turn around and bend over," he breathed out, taking charge.

Quivering in anticipation she did as he instructed, bracing on her elbows and knees as he moved behind her – the sound of his zipper one of the most suggestive things she'd ever heard. Still fully clothed, he sank to his knees behind her, stroking her back and hips, breathing heavily.

"This lingerie is driving me out of my mind. Do you have any idea how sexy you look right now? I could bite your ass it's so perfect."

She gasped as he did just that. She *ached* and her inner thighs clenched attempting to relieve the sweet tension; she was in a sexed-up haze and he hadn't even touched her between her legs.

She needed him inside her. Now. A needy moan fell from her lips.

"Are you ready kitten? Because I don't think I can wait."

Sliding a finger under the edge of her panties he pulled it aside, allowing access to her slick heat. "Oh yeah, you're ready."

Poised at her entrance he paused, and then his thick length plunged inside. She groaned as small stars exploded behind her eyelids. Her head fell forward in a daze of desire and one of his hands cupped a breast, the other holding her hip as he pulled back then thrust forward again.

The sight of his calloused fingers squeezing her flesh was incredibly erotic. Sophie was panting with lust. She needed more.

Now.

She met his next thrust with a backwards one of her own, slamming her body into his. Again with the stars. Perspiration dewed her back as he picked up the pace, now with both his hands gripping her hips so he could control the angle and the rhythm, which was deliciously punishing.

He leant forward over her body so he could bite her neck, "Come for me baby."

Screaming his name, she did.

———

They lay together on their sides with legs tangled, bodies damp with exertion. Steady rain was drumming on the tin roof and Sophie's naked back was pressed against the front of Robert's shirt, his cock still buried inside her. He'd been hard for this every night in that damn hospital.

Lifting her hair from her neck he blew cool air under it. She shivered.

"I think we can call it even now."

She snuggled closer and sighed; "I don't mind if you need to do that again, just to make sure."

He chuckled and came up on an elbow so he could cup her jaw, running his thumb across her kiss-swollen lips. "Next time I might even take the time to get undressed."

"That would be preferable, but I'm not complaining. Any way you want it cowboy."

Lightly smacking her rump he sat up and rolled into a sitting position, before scooping her up and carrying her to the bedroom.

"I see you're taking that literally," she giggled.

Smiling mysteriously he placed her on the bed and left the room.

"Hey! Where do you think you're going?" she called after him playfully.

Heading for his study he felt like beating on his chest in triumph. Sophie was his. They were going to have a baby together. Start a family together. He was a caveman who'd just got his woman. The primal urge to bind them together, officially and forever, rushed unabated through him.

Time in the hospital outside of visiting hours had dripped by interminably, but had allowed him plenty of time to think.

And plan.

Even before Sophie's revelation tonight, he knew he wanted forever with her.

Laptop in hand, he walked quickly back to the bedroom, where she was propped against the bedhead, the sheet loose around her torso, her hair disheveled and her expression curious. At the sight of the laptop she scooted towards him with a grin that was mischievous, if a little wary.

"That looks… kinky."

"You have a filthy mind, you know that?" He sat down beside her and kissed her on the nose, "It's one of things I love about you."

"One of the things huh? Maybe I should get you to list all the rest."

"It's funny you should say that, because I was thinking the same thing. So you know how you gave the PR company the go-ahead to use your photography for the beef collective?"

She eyed him with a puzzled frown, which gave her the most adorable crinkle between her eyebrows. He gave in to the need to kiss it smooth. She pushed him away and shook her head.

"That's a hell of a subject change."

"Bear with me." He opened the laptop and pulled up his email, clicking on the one he wanted. "Well I've been talking with Becky, their media liaison, seeing as I'm the star of the show and all."

She shoved his shoulder, "Let's not forget who made you a star, buster."

He couldn't contain his grin. He was surprised he didn't feel nervous, even though this was the most important thing he'd ever done. Together, they were a sure bet. He just knew it. "At my request they did a second version of the television commercial, which they'll only run the once – tonight."

"Why only run it once? I don't get it."

Opening the email attachment he sat back to watch Sophie's face as the amended version of the commercial promoting their Black Angus cattle began. It opened with one of Sophie's stunning landscape vistas and then rolled into her colour-saturated visual portrayal of life on the land, the voiceover extolling the benefits of farming rich with heritage and tradition, growing wholesome, flavorsome beef.

It ended with a shot of Robert, leaning against a gate with his dusty hat pushed back on his head and a scrolling banner at the bottom of the screen, which read 'Sophie will you marry me?'

Eyes wide, her head snapped up. He slid down to one knee on the floor at her feet, and opened an antique ring box that contained a brilliant Art-Deco diamond engagement ring.

"Sophie, you mean everything to me, and I want forever with you. This ring belonged to my mother, and I know she would have loved for you to have it. Will you wear it and be my wife?"

Sobbing, she flung herself into his arms, gasping "Yes! Yes! Yes!"

Cradling her face in his hands he silenced her with a passionate kiss, sealing their commitment.

"It's the most beautiful thing I've ever seen," she whispered, sliding the ring on to her finger with reverence.

"I think I have to agree," he said, watching the face of the most beautiful thing he'd ever seen.

"Hang on, that's the real commercial? That's going to play on live television?"

"Just the once, at 8.06pm tonight. But I couldn't wait that long to ask you."

"So everyone is going to see you propose to me?" she asked incredulously.

"Well, everyone who's watching television at that time, yes."

"Holy shit."

"And there's number two on the list of things I love about

you – your exquisite use of the English language.”

She grinned cheekily, “Lucky I have the rest of our lives together to add to that list.”

THE END

ACKNOWLEDGEMENTS

I have so much gratitude for my very own tall, dark and handsome man (I can write that, because he'll never read it). We were talking one night about bucket lists, and when I admitted I'd always wanted to write a romance novel, he encouraged me to give it a shot and then supported me (emotionally and financially) while I did. What a man. You rock Wesley Greig.

My thanks to Amy Andrews, who assessed the original manuscript – her insight and experience were invaluable. She (rightly) called bullshit on many, many aspects of the novel and, because of that, this book is 10 times better than it could have been. You should definitely be reading her books.

My besties, Tam Warren and Jill Kelly. We've been tight since we were 15, and they lived the writing of this novel with me. Chapter by chapter, they helped the story unfold. I messaged them the first time I wrote a sentence with the word "quivering" in it, we had a group email to discuss whether boob sex was the done thing now (we decided not), and they have an excellent – and inexhaustible – repertoire of slang words for penis. They have been my biggest cheerleaders and believed even the first draft was brilliant. Bless them.

Thank you to my brother- and sister-in-law, David and Melissa Greig. Mel also had the dubious pleasure of reading my first draft chapter by chapter, and I lived for her encouragement. David was my go-to resource for all things farm-related. I may have spent some of my childhood on a farm, but he's living it day to day, and doing a bloody awesome job. He even took my calls while mustering sheep. Talk about multi-tasking.

Fortunately I have some incredible nurses in my life, my mother-in-law Marg Greig, and friends Amy Smith, Kay Hubbard, Nadine Moxey and Penny Rout. They helped to make Robert's car accident injuries believable (which did mess with my storyline; apparently Robert wasn't going to be sneaking out of hospital with a chest tube in situ. So lucky for him, his diagnosis of a punctured lung was scaled back to just broken ribs!) Side note: it was only Amy Andrews insisting I couldn't get away with this that I changed it, even with the medical knowledge I'd been given, I still wanted to exercise artistic license * insert sheepish expression *

And thank you to my Year Two teacher, Mrs Worthington. I actually hope she doesn't ever read this, because I could never look her in the eye again. But when I was eight she read one of my stories about an alien visiting earth, and thought it was amazing. She believed in my ability and encouraged my love of writing.

ARE YOU READY FOR SARA'S STORY?

GETTING UNDER HER *Skin*

She's single. Looking for Mr Right. And about to have her world turned upside down!

As Beauty Editor for *High Gloss* magazine, Sara Morrison has been known to go to extremes for her job. Doing a podcast while getting a Brazilian wax? Check. But she may have got more than she bargained for when she agreed to get a tattoo for a story. Even if the story is Mitch Smith – Sydney's hottest celebrity tattoo artist. Their instant and undeniable chemistry is about to challenge everything she thought she was looking for.

He was infuriating. An arrogant asshole she could never introduce to her parents. Too bad he had the ability to kiss her senseless.

Recently returned from the States, Mitch's man-whore reputation has followed him home, as has praise for his impressive career trajectory. Not bad for a boy from the wrong side of town. Sara is nothing like the women he usually dates, and Mitch knows he'll never fit into her world. What is it they say about wanting what you can't have?

Just as Sara begins to open herself to the possibility that Mitch could, in fact, be Mr Right, a secret from his past threatens. Can Sara survive the devastating consequences?

Read on for the first chapter of *Getting Under Her Skin*…

CHAPTER 1

"Darling, you know I'm so proud of your career, but I just had lunch with Darla and she said she'd listened to some podcast-thingy of yours. She was shocked, to be honest."

Oh fuck. Sara Morrison gripped her mobile phone tighter. She totally knew where this was going. And really, it had only been a matter of time before someone had made her mother aware of that particular podcast. Darla Simmons would have delighted in being the one to do so, all the while professing her deepest sympathy and concern for Sara's reputation.

If her mother knew she was standing outside a tattoo studio right now for an interview, she'd need her facial botox topped up immediately.

"You were getting waxed," Teresa continued, "down there, and she said it was quite graphic. I knew you didn't just write nice little pieces about Elizabeth Arden lipstick, but it seems like maybe this was, well, going a little too far, frankly. You don't want people to start talking, do you? Especially now that you're seeing Phil – you don't want to jeopardise your relationship by *exposing* yourself like that."

Sara muffled a sigh. Her parents were by and large supportive of her career choice as beauty editor for the fashion magazine *High Gloss*, but she knew they wouldn't blink twice if she married and gave up her job to be a wife and mother. Hell, they expected that, even though she was only 24-years old. Sara wasn't quite sure if her own desire to

Getting Under Her Skin

get married was just a reflection of theirs, and to be honest, she wasn't prepared to look too closely into it. Phil ticked all the right boxes. Except, maybe, for giving her any kind of shivery feelings. But, she reminded herself, they were the stuff of romance novels, not real life.

"Mum, it wasn't that bad. And honestly, Darla isn't exactly the target demographic we were aiming for with that piece."

Sara needed to distract her mother, before she brought her father into the conversation…

"Imagine what your father would say if he knew this is what you were doing with that journalism degree he paid for."

Oh my god.

"Mother, you paid my rent while I was at college – you didn't pay my course fees. I got a scholarship, remember? You make it sound like I didn't earn my degree. And I can't discuss this with you now, because I'm about to do an interview. For my job. So I'll talk to you later. Bye."

She knew that hanging up like that meant she'd have to visit over the weekend to placate her mother – preferably with flowers.

Her job was one area of her life where Sara was free of parental expectations. They didn't feel the need to interfere in something they believed would be short lived. And with time running out to have a career before she married, Sara was desperate to make her mark. Getting a tattoo, however, was maybe going too far.

At last week's editorial meeting, Bridgette, her editor, had given her the opportunity to do a feature on tattoo artist Mitch Smith. Having recently returned from LA, the Aussie-born tattooist had impressive credentials and a swag of celebrity clients singing his praises.

If Sara had to write one more fluff piece waxing lyrical about the perfect shade of blush, she was going to get stabby – she was getting desperate to write something with a little more substance. But writing about an inked, probably uncouth, tattooist wasn't really what she had in mind.

Unfortunately, the celebrity angle appealed to Bridgette. And then Pauline, the heavily pregnant deputy editor, had goaded Sara into actually getting a tattoo, claiming it would add authenticity to the article. Sara was swayed when Pauline proposed the feature could dovetail nicely into a series of syndicated blog posts, giving Sara more coverage.

That, and the fact that Pauline had made an on-the-quiet recommendation for Sara to be her replacement when she left on maternity leave, sealed the deal.

So here she was in the back of a taxi, having sold her soul for the chance at a career promotion and delaying the inevitable.

"Are you getting out love? This is it, PACIFIC at 180 Campbell Parade," said the elderly cab driver, glancing over his shoulder at her for the second time. She really needed to pay him and get out.

"I know. I live here. In Bondi, I mean," she stalled.

"Right." The driver clearly did not care and was already responding to a radio call about his next fare.

Sighing, Sara paid for the ride with a cab charge supplied by the publishing company and stepped into the late afternoon sunshine, careful to avoid a crowd of loitering teenage hipsters, distracted from their destination by the façade of the newly opened Ink Inc. The level of interest wasn't surprising given the buzz the business had been generating.

Living in Bondi, Sara had watched as the historic Swiss Grand Hotel had undergone a massive redevelopment into PACIFIC, which was now super luxe apartments and a world-class dining and retail precinct, including Ink Inc.

With a prime beachfront location and an industrial Brooklyn vibe, Mitch Smith's tattoo studio looked the goods. As apprehensive as she was about this interview, Sara was equally as intrigued to meet the man behind the ink. She'd done her homework, and the man she'd found online was smoking hot. *Smoking* hot.

It was little wonder that most of the paparazzi-style images had gorgeous women hanging off his arms; his reputation as a charismatic bad boy was well documented.

Realising she was now loitering herself, she rubbed her freshly glossed lips together and straightened her pencil skirt. She looked sharp, and knew it.

It was game time.

Stepping into Ink Inc. she was immediately arrested by a wall of street art – graphic and intricate. It was painted over the exposed brick wall behind the concrete counter top that a served as a front desk, and was a focal point for the raw but sophisticated interior. *High Gloss'* sister publication *High Interiors* would cream their panties over the design of the space, which was uber cool while still boasting a laidback vibe.

The woman behind the counter looked like a 1950s pinup girl, complete with beauty mark sitting just above pouty lips, sailor tat on her arm and an hourglass silhouette accentuated by a cinched in belt.

She waved Sara over with a friendly smile.

"Hello pretty lady. I'm Jennifer, what can I do for you today?"

"I'm here to see Mitch. I'm Sara Morrison from *High Gloss* and I'm interviewing him for an article we're running."

"It's nice to meet you, I'm the one who set up the interview with your assistant. I'm Mitch's business partner," she replied.

"Oh. I didn't know he had a business partner."

"It's only a new arrangement. I'm the brains behind the operation," she winked. "Now you, you look like you've got virgin skin," Jennifer purred.

"I do, and it's going to stay that way for a little bit longer," laughed Sara. "I am going to get a tattoo, but not today - that's for some follow-up blog posts."

"Well that's too bad. The boys here would love to get their hands on that creamy skin of yours. Mmmm…" Jennifer mused, running a lacquered nail down a schedule on the laptop. "Mitch is just finishing up with a client now, and I thought I'd slotted you in afterwards… but he's got himself clocking out for the afternoon."

She looked up and grinned at Sara, "but seeing as I'm good at bossing the boss, I'll make it happen."

As she spoke, the door to one of what appeared to be several private tattoo rooms opened and two men came out, laughing and chatting.

"Thanks man. Seriously, this looks amazing – way better than I imagined. I'm stoked."

"Happy to have had the opportunity to work on you. I haven't done Japanese art in a while, I might have to get myself another dragon – it's a timeless piece."

They did the manly back slap thing and the client left,

leaving Mitch to amble towards Jennifer, his eyes lazily travelling up and down Sara's body as his lips turned up in a smirk.

He is totally eye fucking me right now.

Sara's throat went dry and her mind blanked. Which made no sense, because she always dressed to impress and was immune to men checking her out. But this man? He had her panties damp.

He was tall and broad, wearing a plain white t-shirt that hugged a muscular chest and tattooed arms. Scruffy, dark blonde hair was offset by designer stubble on chiseled cheekbones, a strong jaw and full, sensuous lips. Lips that quirked up as he registered she was also checking him out.

Photos on the Internet *did not* come close to preparing Sara for the sheer masculinity of this man. For her reaction to him. She was shaken by the frission of desire that fizzed through her just by *looking* at him.

On her quest for The One she'd been on a relentless schedule of dating that meant she'd been on dates with half of Sydney's male population. Before Phil, none made it past the third date. So yeah, she was a seasoned pro at meeting men. But she'd never known herself to have a physical reaction like this.

What was she, a schoolgirl?

Shaking herself mentally she took a determined step forward with an outstretched hand.

"Hi, I'm Sara Morrison from *High Gloss*."

"And what can I do for you, Sara Morrison from *High Gloss*?" he drawled without a hint of recognition, stepping so close that Sara was inches from his rock-hard body. She could practically feel the heat radiating off him.

Being in such close proximity meant Sara had to look up, way up, to see his face and her traitorous legs went a bit shaky. Dear god he was perfection.

Until he opened his mouth.

"I think I'm going to marry you."

———

What the fuck had he just said?

He should try and take it back, but he was unable to move. He breathed in deep. Damn she smelled good - warm tones of wood and amber. He wanted to lick her neck. Hell, he wanted to lick her everywhere.

She was not his usual type. He liked chicks with an edge; bold and brash rockabilly girls, or the model-types that were there for a good time, not a long time. This one? Yeah. She clearly came from money. She was polished and confident, perfect makeup and not a single hair out of place. An ice princess. And *fuck* he wanted to make her melt and muss up all that perfect hair.

Seeing the faint red glow on her cheeks, he bent down, whispering just an inch from her pretty, shell-like ear, "I bet I could make you blush all over, Princess."

"Are you serious?" she spat, shaking back sleek, ashy blonde hair. "I'm here to interview you, you jerk."

"Interview me?" he ran a hand absentmindedly through his already disheveled hair. Oh yeah, he did remember that. He'd cancelled it on his schedule but forgotten to tell Jennifer about it. She was going to be pissed.

Media coverage about the business was fine, but he wasn't

Getting Under Her Skin

keen on a feature article that was about him. He didn't hide his impoverished childhood, but he sure as hell didn't mention it, either. And there was a little too much dirt in his past for a journalist to be digging around in, thanks anyway.

"We scheduled on Monday, but I'm guessing you've forgotten."

She was cute when she was pissed. Who knew ruffling the feathers of this little princess could be such a turn on?

Get her huffy and she crosses her arms and they push up those amazing tits… interesting.

Whatever. He wasn't doing the interview and she wasn't his type. Not going there.

"Yeah, about that. I'm going to have to cancel. Personal interviews aren't really *my* thing," he gave her a faux apologetic look.

"Well, being unprofessional isn't really my thing. You committed to this interview and we've already reserved pages in the next issue and booked advertising based on the article," she narrowed her eyes at him, long inky lashes sweeping against high cheekbones.

Were her eyes violet? They were hot as fuck, but couldn't be real.

"So how about you get your shit together and reschedule an interview for when it's *convenient* for you," she suggested, those violet eyes staring directly into his.

His cock twitched at her feisty attitude. That perfect creamy skin of hers was flushed and damn if he didn't want to see if he could get her to flush all over. He took a deliberate step forward to crowd her personal space, daring her to back down. She didn't.

He'd bet money that getting inappropriate would be

enough for her to walk away. He was doing her a favour, what did it matter that he was going to have fun doing it?

"Is that what you really want, Princess? Want to spend some time with me, get up close and personal? I seem to remember something about inking you as part of the deal, and I've got to tell you, I can't wait to get under that skin of yours."

Her breathing hitched and he could swear her pupils were dilated in lust. Making women feel this way wasn't new to him, but liking the effect so much was a novelty – maybe LA hadn't jaded him as much as he'd thought.

"You're doing the interview, Mitch," Jennifer said grimly from the reception desk. She'd just hung up the phone and tuned into the conversation.

Ah fuck.

"I have plans right now," he shot back at Jennifer.

Glaring, she turned to address Sara. "Sorry to have inconvenienced you, Mitch can be a dick sometimes," she said sweetly. "He's definitely doing the interview. Any chance you could fit him in tomorrow?"

He saw the ice princess hesitate. He knew he'd pissed her off, but she still wanted the interview.

"He can come to you," Jennifer rushed on. "Whatever's easiest."

Nodding her agreement, Sara startled when the door opened and a leggy brunette waltzed in.

"Oh god, the traffic is a *nightmare* at the moment! So sorry I kept you waiting," she cried, ignoring Sara and Jennifer and draping herself over Mitch. "I can't wait to pick up where we left off last night," she said suggestively, pulling his head down to lock lips.

It was a sexy, open-mouthed kiss, and completely inappropriate for the present situation. Compounding the awkwardness, for the life of him he couldn't remember her name. To be honest, what he'd really been looking forward to this afternoon was hitting the beach.

Since when would I rather surf than tap a fine ass like this?

Since Sara stood glaring at him, those violet eyes flashing. Damn, if looks could kill, he'd be a bloody mess on the floor. He disentangled himself from Mandy. Or was it Miley? Michelle?

He was really setting the asshole bar high today.

"Just give me a second, okay?" he set Mandy/Miley/Michelle aside and tried to get Sara to meet his gaze. Yeah, she was pissed.

"So, tomorrow?"

"Fine. I'll have my assistant email the details."

And she was gone, swishing that rich-girl hair and sashaying those long, long legs. Legs that he'd like to have wrapped around his waist right about now.

"Did you have to be such an assshole?" reprimanded Jennifer, looking up from the computer and giving him a narrow look. "This is going to be good for business Mitch. I need you on your best behavior."

"Yes ma'am."

ABOUT THE AUTHOR

Jacqueline picked up her first Mills & Boon novel when she was 14, and fell head over heels in love with the romance of a happily-ever-after. *Sweet Valley High* just couldn't compete after she got hooked on dashing heroes and plucky heroines.

She has a Bachelor Degree in Print Journalism but, having always been tempted to embellish the facts of a story, decided she was more suited to writing works of fiction. She writes in between wrangling two daughters and my very own tall, handsome husband. *wink wink*

For more on Jacqueline, you can find her at:
www.jacquelinehayley.com
www.instagram.com/jacquelinehayleyromance
www.twitter.com/JHromance
www.facebook.com/jacquelinehayleyromance

A note from Jacqueline...

Thank you for reading my book - it would be amazing if you could take the time to let me know your thoughts…

Not only will this let me know what you feel about my writing, but potential readers will also value your feedback.

If you have bought this book from Amazon you will already have an account that will enable you to review books that you have bought, or have been given as a gift.

If you purchased via iBooks, you can search for Anything But Love and leave your review under the 'Reviews' tab (you need to include a title in order to submit the review)

Goodreads is an excellent site for readers and you can sign in with Facebook or sign up with an email address. This gives you access to thousands of books, enables you to connect with readers of the genres you enjoy, and leave reviews on any books that you have read and feel you would like to offer constructive comments. www.goodreads.com

What will really help me in my future writing is to know some of the following in your review.
1   What did you like or dislike about the style of writing?
2   What did you enjoy about the plot?
3   How did you feel about the main characters?
4   What were your feelings when you finished the book?
5   Anything else that you feel it is important to mention for the benefit of other readers
6   Would you recommend the book to others?

Thank you so much for taking the time to leave a review.
xxx

www.ingramcontent.com/pod-product-compliance
Lightning Source LLC
Chambersburg PA
CBHW071517110726
47908CB00003B/871